THE PROMISE OF A KISS

K. C. BATEMAN

For my three bad rats,
and M, with love.

THE PROMISE OF A KISS

CHAPTER 1

*L*ondon, April 1815.

"I won't do it."

Harry Tremayne, second son of the Earl of Ashton and former cavalryman of His Majesty's Horse Guards, flicked the corner of his newspaper back up and tried to ignore his Great Aunt Agatha, who loomed in front of him.

He failed. The Dowager Countess of Ashton was a woman impossible to ignore, despite being scarcely five feet tall. She was a formidable presence; even her closest friends referred to her as a 'battle ax.'

"You have to go and find her. She's your cousin," Aunt Agatha bellowed.

Harry scowled and lowered the corner of the *Racing Post* again.

"She is *not* my cousin," he said testily. "She's your sister's step-grand-daughter once removed, or something equally convoluted.

I'm more closely related to the king of England. I owe her no familial duty whatsoever."

Aunt Agatha sent him a piercing glare. That look had been very effective when Harry was a boy of seven. It was almost as terrifying now, despite him being twenty years older.

"Well, be that as it may, Henry George Bernard Tremayne," Aunt Agatha said—and Harry knew she was serious, because she'd used his full name—"you owe a duty to *me*. I am old and frail and—"

Harry snorted. "What rot! You're the sprightliest old bird I ever met."

"I'm eighty-one—"

"No, you're not. You're seventy-three. I've seen your birthday in the front of the family bible. And you're as tough as old boots," Harry finished, unmoved. "Send someone else. I've rescued that woman enough times as it is. I spent three years keeping an eye on her in almost every major city in Europe before I went off to serve King and country."

Aunt Agatha opened her mouth, but Harry wasn't finished.

"Lady Hester Morden has an uncanny ability to find areas of the world embroiled in political strife. She is a magnet for trouble. At first I thought she was just unlucky to stumble into such unfortunate situations, but then I realized the truth; Lady Hester is usually the *cause* of said strife."

Aunt Agatha tried to interrupt, but Harry held up his hand.

"She is one of those infuriatingly independent women who drive sane men to drink. She is disaster with a capital D." He raised his eyebrows. "You want to locate her? That's easy; just look at a newspaper. Find somewhere with a peasant uprising or a nasty revolution, and ten to one *she* will be there in the middle of it. Instigating."

He shook his head and adopted an expression of mock regret. "I'm sorry, Aunt Agatha, but I don't want to push my luck. I returned from the wars with barely a scratch. The last time I saw

Lady Hester, she threatened to castrate me. Or shoot me. Or strangle me. Or possibly all three at once."

"That's because you kissed her!" Aunt Agatha boomed, finally managing to get a word in edgeways. "Two years ago. At Lady Bressingham's garden—"

"I had to do *something* to stop her insulting the Turkish ambassador. She kept telling him how dreadful his reforms were. It was the only thing I could think of at the time, short of clubbing her over the head and dragging her body into the shrubbery. Which, come to think of it, would have been a better idea."

Harry frowned.

Certainly it would have been better for his sanity. Because he'd dreamed about kissing Lady Hester Morden for years, annoying baggage that she was, and the real thing had been just as spectacular as he'd feared it would be. He'd known it would be trouble to allow himself even a taste of her, but he'd been unable to resist.

Of course, after that very public kiss, he'd quite properly offered to marry her, but Hester had stoutly refused. She cared nothing for the scandal. She'd been about to accompany her eccentric uncle Jasper, an eminent scholar and cartographer, on an extended tour of Egypt.

Harry had been about to leave the country too, to fight the French tyrant Napoleon, so he'd accepted her refusal with outward good grace and quite a bit of inner irritation. Why didn't she want to marry him? He was a good catch, wasn't he? He had a title, if not a vast fortune, and Hester was an heiress in her own right; she didn't need to marry for money.

He reminded himself he'd had a lucky escape. He hadn't been ready to settle down, and he might have been killed in battle and left her a widow. Hester, too, had craved adventure. Since Egypt was far away from the European war zones, Harry had hoped the trip might keep her out of trouble—at least until he returned from the wars and they could continue their delightful sparring.

He should have known better. Of *course* she'd managed to get herself into some scrape, even with her uncle's supervision. The woman was a menace. And yet he was helpless to resist her. Witness the fact that he'd spent the last few weeks organizing his own passage to Egypt, ostensibly to collect some mummies to sell to the Royal College of Surgeons, but in reality because it was high time someone made sure Hester Morden was still alive.

He shouldn't care if she'd got herself locked away in a harem or robbed by highwaymen. She wasn't his problem. But if he *was* in Egypt, he might as well inquire about her whereabouts.

Aunt Agatha seemed to scent victory. "The family is very concerned, Harry. There's been no letter from Jasper for weeks."

"You know how long it takes for correspondence to get here from Egypt. It's probably just been delayed."

Aunt Agatha shook her head. "I want you to find her. It's time she came back to England and settled down."

"You won't get her married off, even if she does come back," Harry said with conviction. "She's completely uncivilized. She once pushed me into a canal in Venice."

"You doubtless deserved it." Aunt Agatha sniffed. "You were always teasing the poor child."

That was true. He'd been mocking Hester's Italian pronunciation at the time, and thwarting the amorous attentions of a fortune-hunting Count. Hester hadn't thanked him for either.

"You're going to Egypt, aren't you?" Agatha barked. "Your mother told me. So it can't be very far out of your way."

"Do you have any concept of how big Egypt is? It's huge. There are literally thousands of places to get lost and stay lost."

Aunt Agatha ignored this logic. "Your mother said you were going to get some of 'em pharaohs."

"Mummies," Harry corrected. "The Royal College of Surgeons wants mummies. For dissection. They'll pay handsomely for well-preserved specimens."

Aunt Agatha gave a sort of bellow through her nose, which

seemed to indicate disgust, but then her rheumy eyes turned sly. "So that's it! Your pockets are to let. What was it, m'boy? Bad run of cards?" She glanced at the *Racing Post*. "Lame horse?"

Harry raised an eyebrow. His elder brother, James, was heir to the Tremayne estates. As the second son, Harry had preferred to join the Army instead of pursuing a career in either the church or academia, but since Napoleon had been packed off to the island of Elba things had grown rather quiet. He'd resigned from the army and received the payout of his officer's commission, but that wasn't enough to sustain him forever. A trip to Egypt would settle his more pressing debts and build up a nice little nest-egg for the future.

"If something's happened to Jasper, the poor child will be defenseless." Agatha sighed dramatically. "She's a damsel in distress."

Harry barely restrained a snort. "Lady Hester Morden is the last person in Christendom who needs saving. She's the most capable woman I've ever met. She'd doubtless refuse my help, even if I offered it. I'm sorry, Aunt Agatha. Nothing could induce me."

"Not even five thousand pounds?" Aunt Agatha said with faux innocence. "I'll pay five thousand pounds to the man who returns her safely to England."

Harry's jaw went slack. He slid his hand into his waistcoat pocket, withdrew his favorite silver hip flask—the one Hester had given him—and took a fortifying swig of brandy.

"Consider me induced."

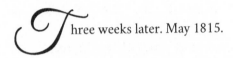hree weeks later. May 1815.

LADY HESTER MORDEN was not having the best day.

She hadn't, in fact, thought it could get much worse after she'd been sneezed on—yet again—by her surly camel, Bahaba, and discovered a scorpion in her boot at breakfast, but the universe was often surprisingly sarcastic. Things, she'd discovered, could *always* get worse.

She'd climbed down into a dry well shaft to examine an interesting series of late Ptolemaic inscriptions she'd glimpsed carved into a panel at the bottom.

Like Uncle Jasper, Hester was a mapmaker, and while her main goal was to complete the definitive map of Upper Egypt they'd come so close to completing before Uncle Jasper's unfortunate death, she was also interested in all forms of ancient archaeology. Maybe she would be the one to crack the mysterious Egyptian picture writing known as hieroglyphics? That would certainly be something.

Determined to get a closer look at the drawings, she'd hitched up her skirts, climbed down the makeshift ladder, and become so absorbed that it was some time before she realized the ladder had been pulled back up.

"Suleiman!" Hester shouted. Her throat was parched from the sand and dust. She was ready for a nice cup of tea in her tent.

But Uncle Jasper's fiercely loyal Mameluke companion, Suleiman, who modestly referred to himself as 'the magnificent', seemed to have disappeared.

Hester frowned. She'd forgotten her hat again, and the sun beat down, remorselessly hot on the top of her head. She shielded her eyes and squinted upwards. "Suleiman! Where the devil are you? Where's the ladder?"

No answer.

Somewhere in the distance a donkey brayed. It sounded a lot like a laugh.

Hester put her hands on her hips and let out a long sigh. Wonderful. Here she was. Stuck at the bottom of a well.

She looked at the curved walls. Perhaps she could climb out? She could wedge her fingers in the gaps between the stones . . . but the thought of the scorpions and snakes that might inhabit those cracks gave her pause.

And then the distinct crunch of footsteps sounded above and she glanced up, her spirits rising. The dark outline of a male figure, just the top half, head and shoulders, bent over the edge of the well and peered down at her.

"Oh, Suleiman. There you are. Thank goodness! Someone seems to have pulled up the ladder without realizing I was down here. Could you get it, please? Or failing that, a rope?"

The sunlight was blinding. Hester squinted upward and frowned. The dark outline, although broad-shouldered, was wearing a European-style hat, not Suleiman's customary turban.

Her stomach dropped. That outline seemed awfully familiar.

No! It couldn't be. Her eyes were playing tricks on her. She hadn't seen *him* for two years. It was a mirage, brought on by too much sun.

She blinked, but the shadow remained.

It was so bright she couldn't see the man's face clearly, but somehow she just *knew* he was laughing at her.

Hester closed her eyes and muttered a fervent prayer to whichever gods might be listening. "Please, no. *Anyone* but him."

If she had to choose the one man in the whole northern hemisphere she never wanted to see again, Harry Tremayne would be that man.

"What are you doing down there?" the shadow called cheerfully, and the sound of that deep, amused voice confirmed her very worst suspicions.

"Harry Tremayne!" she croaked. "What in hell's name are *you* doing here?"

"A delight to see you too, Lady Morden," came the irritatingly upbeat reply.

Hester ground her teeth.

The shadow gave a sarcastic flourish of his hat. "I've come to rescue you."

"You? Rescue *me*? Ha! That's rich."

"I'm not the one stuck at the bottom of a well," he pointed out with irrefutable logic. "You shouldn't be so quick to refuse my assistance. Wait there. I'll get you a ladder."

Within moments the rickety ladder descended into the shaft, and with a sigh of resignation, Hester climbed back out. She ignored the outstretched hand Harry offered her and climbed over the low wall herself, then made a great show of dusting down her skirts to give herself some time before she straightened up to greet her nemesis.

It was just as bad as she'd expected. Harry Tremayne was as heart-stoppingly good looking as ever. His dark, tousled hair screamed for her fingers to touch it. Those taunting blue eyes both mocked and invited at the same time. And he had a pair of lips she'd dreamed about kissing for far too many nights.

He was wearing a thin white shirt tied carelessly at the throat, a pair of buff breeches, leather riding boots, and a leather satchel slung across his chest, bandolier-style. He looked like a pirate, like the charming rogue he was.

Hester narrowed her eyes. She, no doubt, was a dusty, sweaty mess. He *always* managed to catch her at a disadvantage.

"Do you know how many miles there are between here and London, Mr. Tremayne?" she said stiffly.

"Not precisely," he admitted. "A lot."

"If you take the overland route, it's approximately five-and-a-half thousand. As the crow flies, it's a little over two thousand."

He raised one irritatingly perfect eyebrow. "What's your point?"

"That's two thousand marvelous miles I'd put between you, Harry Tremayne, and myself."

He cocked his head and sent her an amused, chiding glance. "You're not still angry about that kiss, are you? Good Lord. I offered to marry you, didn't I? You refused."

"You only offered because you'd ruined my reputation!"

"So? It was the honorable thing to do."

Hester poked him in the chest with her index finger. "*So*, I'm not marrying someone who was forced into it because of some stupid scandal. I want someone who *wants* to marry me."

He shook his head, as if this was mystifying female logic at its worst. "And here I was, thinking you'd be happy to see a familiar face." He clapped his hands over his heart in a theatrical gesture. "I'm wounded, Lady Morden. To the core. One could almost infer you aren't glad to see me at all."

She sent him a stony glare.

He looked around with a sudden frown. "Where's your Uncle Jasper?"

Hester tried not to look guilty. "He's dead, actually."

"Dead! Since when?"

She raised her chin. "Since five weeks ago. He had some sort of apoplexy. It was very sudden. One minute we were surveying the east ridge of the—"

"Five weeks? He's been dead for that long?" Harry interrupted. "And you didn't think to send a letter back to England? Or to return to Cairo and inform the British Consul, Henry Salt?"

"No, I did not. Because I knew that as soon as I did, everyone would demand I come home. I'm not ready. I decided to stay and finish Uncle Jasper's map of Upper Egypt instead. It's what he would have wanted. I'm nearly done, in fact. I only need a few more days."

Harry's expression portrayed his shock and annoyance. "Good God. It's a miracle you're still alive. You've been out here all alone, unprotected—"

"Hardly," Hester scoffed. "I have Suleiman. He's a trained bodyguard. A Mameluke soldier who once guarded Ali Pasha himself."

Harry placed his hands on his hips. "So where is he?"

"I don't know, actually. It's most unlike him to simply disappear."

Harry rolled his eyes.

"In any case," Hester continued, "I also have a letter of protection from Muhammad Bey himself. It gives me free, unencumbered passage throughout his empire and promises dire consequences for anyone who interferes with me or my retinue."

"Oh, and I'm sure any bandit's going to take the time to read a *letter* before he robs and murders you," Harry drawled. "How did you get such a thing, anyway?"

"Uncle Jasper and the Pasha were good friends. We stayed at the palace for a few weeks when we first arrived in Alexandria, and I became quite fond of his wives. They loved hearing stories about England. I gave one of them a simple remedy to treat her head cold and the Bey gave Uncle Jasper the letter of protection in thanks."

Harry sent her a frustrated look. "You need a man to protect you out here, not a bit of paper. Egypt's not safe for a woman alone. Even one as intrepid as you."

"Oh, pah. Everyone I meet out here regards me as a curiosity. There's really no need for you to be here. I'll make my own way back to England in my own time."

"There's every need."

Hester glared at him. "Why are you *really* here, Tremayne?"

"Well it's certainly not for the pleasure of your so-charming company. I'm doing this as a favor to my Aunt Agatha. She insisted someone came and collected you."

"I'm not a parcel!" Hester fumed. "And I don't believe you. You never do anything out of the goodness of your heart."

"Well, if you want to know the truth, it's for the money."

"What money?"

Harry grinned—that gorgeous, boyish, wicked grin that did funny things to her insides.

"There's a price on your head. A bounty, if you will. Aunt Agatha's offered five thousand pounds to the man who returns you safely to England."

"She did not!"

"She really did. And unlike you, Lady Morden, I'm not in line to inherit a whopping great fortune. Some of us have to make a living. Plebeian concerns, I know, but there you go."

Hester sucked in a deep breath. The scorching desert air burned her lungs. "How could she? And you! You're nothing but a fortune hunter!"

Tremayne didn't even bother to deny it. His shrug was a study in insouciance, and Hester chided herself for noticing the way the thin cotton of his shirt clung lovingly to the muscles of his shoulders. He had a splendid physique, she had to admit. He was almost as broad as Suleiman.

"I was coming this way, anyway," he said. "I want some mummies to take back to the Royal College of Surgeons. They want to dissect 'em."

"You can't do that!"

"I don't believe I require your permission," he said haughtily. "Both you and those mummies are coming back with me to England, whether you like it or not."

Hester opened her mouth to say she'd rather deal with the devil himself, but he held up his hand in a conciliatory gesture.

"Wait! I'll make you a deal. You say you only need another few days to finish your map. I need a few days to procure some mummies. If you promise to behave—and that means no escape attempts and no trying to get rid of me: no snakes in my bed, no scorpions in my breeches, et cetera, et cetera—then I will let you finish your work before we catch a ship back to England."

Hester took a step towards him so they were almost nose to nose. Well, nose to chest; he was a good eight inches taller than she was. She tried not to notice how good he smelled. How was that even possible in this heat? Damn the man.

"I'd rather be eaten by a plague of locusts," she said sweetly. "In fact, given the choice between spending even one day with you or experiencing every one the ancient biblical plagues simultaneously, I'd choose the flies and the frogs without a moment's hesitation. You are a pestilence, Harry Tremayne."

His obnoxious smile only widened at her show of temper.

"If you *don't* agree to behave," he said, equally sweetly, "I will simply roll you up inside a carpet, like Cleopatra when she had herself delivered to Julius Caesar, and transport you to Alexandria on the back of a camel."

He studied her hot face with his wicked gaze for a long moment, and Hester's heart hammered uncomfortably against her throat.

"Do we have a deal?" Tremayne purred.

Hester knew further resistance would be futile. She'd always assumed her family would send someone after her sooner or later, and in truth she'd been surprised it had taken quite so long. Still, she'd enjoyed five whole weeks of extra freedom away from the stuffy drawing rooms of London, which counted as a victory of sorts. It was simply a shame that her escort should turn out to be the one man she'd wanted forever and could never have.

She managed a creditable sigh. "Oh, all right. Deal."

CHAPTER 3

*T*remayne gave a satisfied nod and glanced around them. His brow furrowed. "Where are we, anyway?"

"The Fayium Oasis," Hester sniffed. She pointed to the dusty track that led out into the barren desert as far as the eye could see. "That's the Forty Days Road, the trade route used to transport gold, ivory, spices, and animals for centuries." She frowned. "Surely you've been using a map?"

He shook his head, and she gasped in disapproval.

"No, I simply started in Alexandria, asking after a pair of eccentric Europeans: one gentleman of around sixty years old and a young woman with fair skin and light hair. I followed the gossip here to you. You're really rather unforgettable, Lady Morden."

His eyes swept her in a leisurely perusal that somehow managed to make her feel even hotter and more flustered than ever.

"Being a foreigner, of course," he added belatedly, his eyes alight with teasing.

She inclined her head. "You were extremely fortunate to find us. Although, I'll admit that maps of this region aren't particu-

THE PROMISE OF A KISS

larly useful. When Napoleon came here fifteen years ago, he brought a whole army of cartographers to make more accurate ones, but they lost most of their precision instruments when the ship carrying them sank on the way from France. The best map currently available is more than thirty years old—which is why it's so important that I finish the one started by Uncle Jasper."

Tremayne rolled his eyes and pointed toward the well-preserved ruins of a fort on a nearby hill. "What's that?"

"The Romans built a string of fortresses to protect the trade caravans from attack."

"I was told they used to send ruffians out here. The Egyptian equivalent of transportation to the Antipodes. Seems fitting *you* should end up here."

Hester ignored the jibe. "Indeed. The practice of using the place as a colony for exiles continued well into the Christian era. It became a refuge for hermits who lived in isolated tombs or caves." She waved toward the rocky outcrops that surrounded the oasis.

Tremayne cocked a brow. "A life spent far away from interfering women. I can see the appeal."

She gave an inelegant snort. "As if you could abstain from female company for more than a week, Tremayne."

Back in England his reputation was that of a charming rogue. Women, especially beautiful widows, had always thrown themselves at him, drawn to his sinful good looks and quick wit. His supposed prowess in the bedroom was legendary. *He'd doubtless found himself a mistress the minute he'd returned from the wars,* Hester thought crossly. Not that she cared. Harry Tremayne's personal life was none of her business.

She glanced around to avoid looking at his too-handsome face. The oasis was actually rather picturesque. The shocking green of the date palms was a welcome contrast to the barren, stony desert all around. But for the first time, she became aware of how very remote it was. Where *was* Suleiman?

Only a handful of permanent settlers lived in the ramshackle cluster of houses nearby. They tended the narrow strip of fertile land that surrounded the water-filled depression in the sand and shepherded goats through the surrounding hills. She and Tremayne were probably the only Europeans within a hundred-mile radius.

If she'd had a reputation to lose, being alone with him here would have ruined her utterly, but she was already beyond the pale—thank goodness—and they were far from the preposterous rules and regulations of the *ton*.

A handsome Arabian stallion and a bored-looking donkey laden with colorful packs had been tied to a nearby date palm: presumably Tremayne's transport.

"I hope you've brought sufficient supplies for yourself," Hester said crossly. "There certainly isn't room for you in *my* tent."

He sent her an innocent grin. "I never thought there would be. Don't worry about me. I'm quite used to sleeping out in the open. And since your bodyguard seems to have to deserted you, I'll gallantly position myself outside your tent to protect you from any unwanted intruders."

"To make sure I don't sneak off in the night, more like," Hester countered bitterly.

He leaned back against the low stone wall of the well. "That too. Now, I'm sure you'd like to show your gratitude for my rescuing you."

He ignored her snort and pointed at the haphazard ruins that littered the hillside. "We still have a few hours left before sunset. Why don't you show me some nice tombs where I can find a mummy or two? The locals assure me there are plenty left, even if the other grave goods were looted centuries ago. I spoke to a chap named Mehmet on the way here, who said his brother recently discovered the entrance to a new tomb while searching for a lost goat."

Hester shook her head. "Why do you need to find one yourself? Why not just *buy* a mummy if you're so keen to have one? I distinctly remember seeing any number of sarcophagi being offered for sale in antique shops in Cairo."

"Most of those were simply the decorated wooden cases. The good physicians of London want bodies. And, besides, I was warned against fake mummies in Alexandria. Some unscrupulous dealers use recently deceased convicts, apparently. They cover them in tar, leave them to dry in the sun, then wrap them up in bandages and sell them to unsuspecting tourists." He straightened and stalked off towards the ruins, his long legs eating up the distance. "No, finding my own is the only way to guarantee what I have is authentic. Come on."

Hester was tempted to ignore him but then decided she might as well try to dissuade him from his distasteful task. She did *not* approve of removing mummies from their eternal resting place. It would serve him right if he fell into a burial shaft and cracked his handsome head open.

She lifted her skirts and hurried after him. "There are bats inside many of the tombs, you know," she called. "Some of them are the size of pigeons."

He glanced over his shoulder and cocked a brow in challenge. "Scared, Morden?"

"Of course not! I've learned to deal with all manner of annoying vermin out here." She paused meaningfully and hoped he caught the insult. "I was merely concerned for *you.*"

She heard him chuckle. "It won't be the first time we've ever been in a tomb together, will it? What about Paris? The cata-combs? I rescued you then, too."

"You did not. I knew exactly where I was. You gave me the fright of my life, sneaking up on me like that!"

He chuckled again. "The moment is etched into my memory. The way you clutched at me in fright, you almost leapt into my arms—"

"What rot!"

"Your breasts were plastered against my chest. Your arms were around my neck—"

"If my arms were around your neck, Tremayne, I was trying to throttle you."

Hester did her best to ignore the uncomfortable flush that heated her face and the thrill of remembered sensation that swept down her body. He was only teasing her. The man just lived to shock. He couldn't possibly know how many times she'd relived that moment of being in his arms—albeit temporarily— since then. Or how she'd obsessed over their one glorious, unexpected kiss.

They reached the edge of the village and started to pick their way between the domed mudbrick mausoleums and ruined walls of the ancient settlement that covered the hillside. Hester had already explored the area on several occasions, although she'd never done more than peer into the entrances of the many pit graves and necropolises. One chapel she'd discovered had been almost intact, with the most beautiful drawings decorating the walls. Uncle Jasper had thought it dated back to the reign of the Persian ruler Darius.

Tremayne bounded athletically between the huge tumbled stone blocks. The remains of a temple of some sort: twelve palm-columns with stylized tulip-shaped tops lay at odd angles amid the sandy rubble. He glanced back at her, and she reluctantly accepted his outstretched hand to clamber over a particularly large boulder.

His hand was so much larger than hers, long fingered and strong, and she let go as quickly as possible.

"I know you disapprove of me taking mummies back to England," he said cheerfully, "but it's hardly a new phenomenon. King Charles the second used to collect the dust from them to use on his skin. He believed the 'greatness' would rub off on him."

"That's ridiculous."

"I've also heard of people grinding them into powder to cure all kinds of illnesses."

Hester made a face. "Ugh. That's almost as bad as the Ancient Egyptians. You wouldn't believe some of the things they used as medicine. A bag of mouse bones fastened round the neck, for example, was a cure for bed-wetting."

Tremayne gave a bemused chuckle. "*Please* use that as a conversation starter when we're back in England. I can't wait to see the stunned reactions."

Hester ignored him. "Ingredients were often selected because they came from a plant or animal that had characteristics which corresponded to the symptoms of the patient. So they would use an ostrich egg for the treatment of a broken skull, or wear an amulet of a hedgehog to ward against baldness."

She glared at the back of Tremayne's perfect head. He had no need of a hedgehog amulet. His hair was thick and dark, with a slight wave that always made her want to run her fingers through it. Curse him.

She cleared her throat. "They had some very odd notions regarding anatomy, too. The brain was considered relatively unimportant—as evidenced by the fact that it was usually discarded during the mummification process."

She wrinkled her nose at his broad back. "Actually, they may have been on to something there. I can think of several people whose brains could be removed and one would fail to see a noticeable difference."

If Tremayne registered her veiled insult, he didn't rise to the bait. He merely ducked inside one of the small tombs that backed onto the hillside. Hester followed, blinking as her eyes adjusted to the darker interior.

The back wall of the tomb was built into the bedrock, and Harry smiled as he spied an opening in the craggy rock face, partly covered with a plank of wood. He shifted the wood and uncovered a dark tunnel that seemed to lead straight into the hill itself.

"Ha!" he shouted in triumph. "Look at that! I bet that goes down to a burial chamber of some sort. Come on."

"Don't be ridiculous. You can't go down there. For one thing we have no light."

He sent her a chiding glance, reached into the leather satchel slung across his chest, and pulled out two candles and a tinder box. The flint sparked as he lit the candles and handed one to her with a grin. *Semper Paratus*. That's the Tremayne family motto. It means 'Always prepared.' We Tremaynes are ready for anything."

"The Morden family motto is *Non Perdidi*."

"'Never lost,'" Tremayne translated. "An excellent motto for a family of mapmakers." His smile made her stomach flutter. "Come on. Let's go."

And before Hester could argue, he'd bent over and started down the dark, narrow passageway.

CHAPTER 4

*F*or want of anything better to do, Hester followed him, cursing under her breath as she did so. The candlelight flickered on the rough-hewn walls of the tunnel as it sloped gradually downward. The air was cool in contrast to the scorching heat outside and slightly musty. After approximately twenty feet Tremayne stopped to clear some rocks and other debris out of their path, but once that was done, he continued on, humming a rather tuneless ditty that made Hester grind her teeth.

The idiot was enjoying himself.

Hester did her best to ignore the crushing feeling of knowing they were surrounded by hundreds of tons of rock that might collapse on top of them at any moment. She was finding it hard to breathe in the airless space. Her chest felt tight. She took a deep breath—and inhaled the intoxicating scent of Harry Tremayne.

My goodness, he smelled good. The faint tang of cedar and leather made her stomach curl. Why couldn't he smell all sweaty and dusty, like a normal person?

"The ancient Egyptians liked to set booby traps," she warned, her voice echoing strangely off the narrow walls.

"Really? Like what?" His voice was more eager than fearful, the dolt.

"There might be other shafts for you to fall down or stones triggered by wires to crush you. If you die, Tremayne, don't think I'm going to drag your mangled body out of here. I'll think of some excuse to tell your Aunt Agatha."

His amused laughter echoed back to her.

After another fifty feet or so, his silhouette straightened and then disappeared. Hester hastened forward and emerged into a small rectangular chamber that had been hewn into the solid rock. It wasn't much larger than a closet or a dressing room. A few small alcoves and recesses had been carved into the walls, but whatever treasures they'd once held were long gone.

She raised her candle and made a slow turn around the chamber. Each wall was covered in a series of beautiful Egyptian paintings, the colors of which were still remarkably bright and well-preserved. She sucked in an awed breath at the stylized human figures, plants, and animals that seemed to fill every available space.

"Well, that's quite something," Harry breathed.

He stepped forward and peered into the large stone trough that stood in the center of the room. It had obviously once had a lid, but the shattered remains of it lay strewn on the floor.

"Empty," he sighed. "If there was a mummy in there, it's long gone."

"Probably a good thing," Hester said. "It would doubtless have been cursed. The ancient Egyptians were always putting curses on things." She gestured at the lines of picture writing that decorated all four sides of the sarcophagus. "That probably says something like, 'Cursed be he who moves my body. To him shall come fire, water, and pestilence. His liver shall be eaten by a crocodile.

His neck shall be twisted like that of a bird. His name shall cease to exist.'"

Harry made a dismissive noise. "Ha. There's no such thing as curses. A man makes his own luck. I discovered *that* in the wars. Mind you, it does show how very uncreative we British are when it comes to insults. All we do is sneer at the cut of a man's coat or disparage his sister. I'm going to memorize some of those, to use when I'm back home."

Hester rolled her eyes. "Well, if you're quite satisfied there's nothing left to steal down here, perhaps we can make our way back?"

"Steal?" Harry protested. "I never steal!"

"Oh, really? What about that time in Venice when you stole that gondola from those nuns?"

He raised his brows. "I prefer the term commandeered. Or borrowed. I *borrowed* that gondola. And in my defense, I had no idea they really were nuns."

"The wimples weren't a sufficient clue? And the rosary beads?"

"It was Carnevale. I thought they were in fancy dress."

"Well, they weren't. They probably told the Pope to excommunicate you."

"It's hardly the worst thing I've ever done," Harry shrugged. "And you got home safely that night, did you not? I was sparing you the attentions of that slimy Count whatever-his-name-was."

"Count Trastevere," Hester sniffed. "And he was charming."

"He was a penniless fortune hunter," Harry said bluntly. "I was helping you as a friend."

Hester showed her teeth in a smile that was almost a snarl. "Why, *thank you*, Tremayne. But I don't recall asking for your interference."

He shrugged again, unimpressed by either her sarcasm or her ire. "You're very welcome."

She turned back towards the tunnel with a frustrated huff.

"You are *so* annoying. I hope your camel bites you. I hope you get eaten by sand flies. I hope a scorpion takes up residence in your unmentionables."

"Now that's just being mean."

A mirthless chuckle escaped her as she started back along the passageway. She could sense him following behind her and instantly wished she'd allowed him to go first so he wouldn't have a close-up view of her posterior.

"I don't know what it is about you," she marveled. "No one else manages to irritate me quite so thoroughly." She stepped briskly over a pile of rubble.

"Have you ever wondered why that is?"

"Why what is?"

"Why I'm the only man who has this effect on you. I've seen you deal with imbeciles back in London with the utmost calm. You suffer fools with a polite smile. But me? I drive you crazy."

He sounded insufferably pleased.

"I suppose you have some wonderfully enticing theory?" Hester called back along the tunnel. She could see the faint rectangle of light ahead. Almost there.

"I do, as a matter fact."

"I'm all agog to hear it," she said waspishly.

"It's because you have feelings for me."

She almost dropped her candle. "I most assuredly do not!"

"You must have, otherwise you'd have no problem ignoring me, as you do everyone else, or reasoning with me. But I get under your skin. I ruffle your feathers. I alone drive you insane."

Hester stepped out of the tunnel into the tiny mausoleum and straightened. She extinguished her candle then whirled round to face Tremayne as he, too, left the shaft. "You are insufferably conceited."

"And right," he added cheerfully. He blew out his own candle, plunging them into shadow, and took a step toward her.

Suddenly the small room seemed smaller. Hester could feel her heart racing madly against her ribs.

He raised his brows at her in mocking challenge. "Admit it. You like me. I might even go as far as to suggest that you *desire* me."

"Desire you?! Ohh! You deluded—"

He moved closer still, and a mocking smile curved the corner of his lips. "Let's test my theory, shall we? If, as you claim, I have no effect on you, then I should be able to kiss you and elicit no response whatsoever, except revulsion. Or boredom."

Hester could barely breathe. What game was he playing now? Why was he taunting her like this? She should call his bluff. She should kiss him and stay as still as a statue, as unmoved as one of the carvings that adorned the temples by the Nile.

But then she remembered the last time he'd kissed her, two years ago, and all hope of remaining unaffected fled. Just the thought of it made her stomach coil in excitement. If he kissed her now, she'd embarrass herself by responding. It would mean nothing to him, of course. It would be a game, a tease. But it would mean everything to her. He could never know just how much she wanted him.

"Kiss me," he murmured.

He leaned in, but she turned her head so his lips only grazed her cheek. Even *that* brief contact was enough to make her pulse accelerate and her knees go a little wobbly. She stepped back with what she hoped was an easy laugh.

"I'll kiss you the day it rains in the desert, Harry Tremayne. Which is to say, never."

She turned and escaped out into the afternoon heat. The sun dazzled her eyes.

Tremayne followed. He glanced up at the cloudless azure sky and smiled. "I'll hold you to that."

She sent him a smug look. "It hasn't rained here for over a hundred years. It would be nothing less than a miracle."

She turned to go back down the hill, but the glint of something metallic in the sand caught her eye. She poked it with the toe of her boot, and the glitter of silver flashed in the sun. She bent down to examine it further.

"What's that you've found?"

"I'm not sure."

She tried to pick it up, then snatched her hand back as her fingers touched the gleaming metal. It was burning hot—presumably from being out in the sun all day. More cautiously, she brushed the sand aside, exposing the object. A red stone flashed, like a tiny drop of blood, and to her amazement a chain, followed by some kind of jeweled pendant, emerged from the sand.

Hester stared at it, her heart racing. The thing was undoubtedly ancient, although she wasn't sure how she knew that. Perhaps because the design was oddly seductive.

She lifted the thing fully free of the sand. The pendant was shaped like a scorpion gripping the silver chain in its pincers. One large cabochon ruby was set in the center of its back, and smaller gems glittered along the slender curve of its tail. It was extremely realistic, almost life-size, and Hester gave a shiver of fascinated revulsion. The reticulated silver sections of the body and tail allowed it to move; it undulated sinuously with the faint tremor of her hand.

It seemed ridiculous to think of a piece of jewelry as *threatening*, but for some reason the description fit. She gave herself a mental shake and stood.

"Good heavens. Look at this."

CHAPTER 5

*T*remayne gave a low, impressed whistle. "You have the devil's own luck, Morden. Let me see."

Hester lifted the necklace for inspection. Without thought, she undid the clasp, reached around her nape and put it on. It was surprisingly heavy. The high neck of her cotton dress prevented the hot metal from touching her skin, but she could feel the weight of the pendant pressing against her.

Tremayne reached out a finger and traced the chain across her collarbone. Her breath caught in her throat. He reached the pendant and paused, and Hester was sure he must be able to feel the telltale thundering of her heart through the silver. Intent on his task, he followed the shape of the scorpion's body down, down, flattening the creature's tail against her breastbone. The tip of it, the sting, uncurled to nestle perfectly in the valley at the top of her breasts.

Hester's skin burned. A rush of some strong emotion—anger or passion—flashed through her veins.

"Beautiful," Harry breathed.

He lifted his eyes to hers, and for a split second she glimpsed a depth of feeling that was shocking in its intensity. Was it anguish? *Desire?* His gaze burned into hers, direct and faintly challenging. He parted his lips as if to speak, and Hester leaned toward him, desperate to hear what he was about to say—but a dog barked in the distance, and the odd moment was broken.

He blinked as if coming out of a trance, dropped his hand, and stepped back.

"It suits you." He cleared his throat and sent her an easy smile. "This proves the utter injustice of life. I noticed it during the wars. Brave, decent men got blown to pieces, while others—cowardly, undeserving idiots—dodged bullets time and time again." He indicated the necklace. "This is another example. The universe throws a ridiculously valuable artifact into the path of the one woman in a hundred-mile radius who doesn't need the cash."

Hester unfastened the necklace with a deep feeling of relief, as if a weight had been lifted off her shoulders. She placed it carefully in the pocket of her split skirt.

"What are you going to do with it?" Harry asked casually. "If you sell it, then I should definitely get half the proceeds."

She gave a choked laugh. "And how do you figure that?"

"You would never have been up here if it hadn't been for me. Admit it."

That was undoubtedly true.

"If you give me half the money," he coaxed, "I won't need to sell any mummies. I bet Henry Salt or the British Museum would pay handsomely to add it to their collections."

Hester shook her head. "You're such a jackal. This should stay in Egypt. It's part of the country's heritage. I'm going to hand it over to the Bey himself. He told me he has plans to open some kind of national museum."

Tremayne gave a disappointed sigh. "I'll just have to keep my eye out for some mummies, then." He laughed at her frown as he stepped past her and started down the hillside. "You have no right to look so disapproving. I'm only a second son. I've left it a bit late to become a doctor or a tutor. And I doubt I'll be allowed to join the clergy—remember the Venetian nuns?"

"That's what the marriage mart is for," Hester said lightly, ignoring the twinge that pierced her heart. "You need to find yourself a nice, rich heiress. Some sweet, biddable thing who covets the illustrious Tremayne ancestry."

He sent her a lopsided smile. "Tried that. The last heiress I asked to marry me turned me down flat."

She tried not to wince.

"That was you, by the way," he added unnecessarily.

As if she needed clarification. "I'm hardly the biddable sort," she said tartly. "I'm nothing like the fashionable women of the *ton*. I am freckled—"

"Sun-kissed," he amended.

"With sun-bleached hair—"

"It's golden. Honey and copper."

"Oh."

Hester stammered to a stop. Tremayne always managed to do this to her, to leave her bemused and tongue-tied. He flirted so effortlessly; it was as natural to him as breathing. He probably flirted with his donkey when there were no other females around. And yet he seemed to like—appreciate, even—all the qualities she herself disliked. He was a singularly unusual man.

Why hadn't he married? He was certainly a catch. A tall, dark, handsome, titled Adonis who also happened to be funny, kind, and incredibly alluring. Any woman would be desperate to have him.

Hester glanced at his profile. It was like gazing at one of the statues of the great pharaohs, all straight lines and attractive masculine angles. She wondered what he'd look like in just a pleated loin-cloth, bare-chested, and a hot flush warmed her skin.

He could be as autocratic as a pharaoh, too, she reminded

herself sternly. He just loved bossing people around, having everyone jump to do his bidding.

"You won't have any problem finding a husband when we're back in England," he said abruptly. "With your fortune, any number of men will be willing to overlook your unfashionably tanned skin and your even more unfashionable intelligence."

"Who says I *want* a husband?" Hester said crossly. "What use are they?"

His smile was entirely too wicked. "Oh, I daresay they have their occasional uses."

She refused to rise to the bait. He was, presumably, referring to a husband providing amorous services, but she was well aware one didn't need to be married for *that*. The Bey's concubines had been most instructive on the matter.

"Actually, come to think of it, you don't need a husband," he said. "You need a keeper. Like the wild animals at the zoo. Someone to steer you away from—"

"Stop!" Hester croaked. "Hold right where you are, Tremayne."

Thankfully, he did as he was told. He froze, just as she had done, and swiveled his gaze downward to see what commanded her attention.

A cobra, a dark, deserty brown, swayed back and forth on a sandstone block within striking distance of his foot. Its hood was extended. A warning hiss issued from its fanged mouth.

"Don't move," Hester whispered urgently.

"Can it bite me through my boot?" Harry whispered back.

"Do you really want to find out?"

With almost imperceptible slowness, she stretched her hand toward a loose piece of masonry about the size of her fist. The movement caught the snake's attention. It turned its body away from Tremayne, just as she'd intended, and fixed its malevolent glare on her. Quick as a flash, she grabbed the rock and hurled it at the snake.

The serpent appeared to jump into the air as the fragment hit its body. It made a lightning-fast turn and disappeared into the gap between two blocks.

Hester let out a relieved breath then shot a slack-jawed Tremayne a cocky look.

"Good shot," he breathed with genuine admiration.

She decided there was no need to reveal how surprised *she* was at her uncharacteristic accuracy. It was as if she'd been bestowed with supernatural powers.

She raised her brows. "You were saying something about me needing a keeper? As you can see, I don't need *any* man's protection."

"I take it all back," he said with a chuckle. "You are a fully independent, snake-battering virago. Come on, let's go and have a cup of tea."

"We ran out of tea about six months ago," Hester said, hurrying after him. "There's only the mint tea the locals drink."

That was one thing she'd missed about England: not the rainy climate, but black tea with cow's milk and a decadent spoonful of sugar.

They reached the clearing with her well and his horse. Tremayne untied the panniers from the donkey, untethered both animals, and glanced around. "So, where have you made camp?"

Hester led him around the back of a partly-ruined temple to where she and Suleiman had pitched their tents and smiled at the sight of the colorful striped material.

Uncle Jasper hadn't believed in traveling light. He'd been loath to give up his creature comforts, even when traveling so far from home, and his 'essential items' had included a full Meissen tea service, a campaign-style folding bed with feather bedroll, a portable writing slope, and numerous woolen rugs to protect the feet from the sandy, rocky ground. It wasn't Grosvenor Square levels of luxury, but it wasn't entirely uncomfortable.

Tremayne made short work of starting a fire, and Hester tried not to be impressed. She doubted the Harry Tremayne she'd known three years ago would have been able to do that. He'd lived for pleasure, not practicality. Now he was indisputably a soldier, older and wiser, with a competence to match. He was a little bit more wicked too, and the additional lines around his eyes and the hint of grey at his temples only added to his unholy appeal. This Harry Tremayne was a man, not a boy.

But still not the man for her.

He bent and rummaged in one of the saddlebags. "I brought you a present. All the way from England."

Hester accepted it gingerly and untied the string that bound the brown paper. The scent hit her first, and she took a deep, appreciative sniff then almost squealed in delight. "Oh, my! Black tea? Thank you."

She smiled at him with genuine pleasure. His gaze dropped to her mouth, and she experienced a squirming sensation low in her belly. She bit her lip, and he glanced up with a wry expression.

"You're welcome. It was Aunt Agatha's idea, actually."

"Well, there's no milk, I'm afraid. Unless you want camel milk?"

"No, thank you."

Hester marveled at the strangeness of politely taking tea with Harry Tremayne in the middle of the desert. It was bizarre, almost like a dream, and yet it somehow seemed entirely natural. As if she'd always imagined him here with her.

She frowned. "I am becoming increasingly concerned about Suleiman. It's very unlike him to simply disappear without a word. What if he's been injured? He could have fallen into a burial shaft or been bitten by a snake or a scorpion."

"Perhaps we should ask the locals?"

"Most of them are tending to their sheep in the hills. But there is one village elder who might know where he is."

"Let's go see him, then. And perhaps he can tell us more about that necklace, too."

CHAPTER 6

The Fayium village elder was an ancient, wizened old man whose face was the color and wrinkled texture of a ripe date. Hester and Tremayne ducked into his ramshackle hut and accepted a seat, cross-legged on the floor.

The old man spoke a smattering of both English and French, having served for some time as a translator for Napoleon's invading army, but the clarity of his speech was hampered by the fact that he lacked most of his teeth. With halting gestures and a good deal of pantomiming, they finally deduced that no-one had seen Suleiman since earlier that afternoon, when he'd watered Bahaba, Hester's bad-tempered camel.

When Hester reached inside her pocket and withdrew the scorpion necklace, the old man sucked in an awed breath. His gnarled fingers shook as he reached out to touch it, then he seemed to change his mind and snatched his hand away. He made a gesture in the air, as if to ward off evil.

"Where it find you?" he asked urgently. "Here?"

Hester frowned. "Do you mean, 'where did I find it?'"

The old man shrugged, as if it were the same thing.

"Up on the hill, in the sand outside one of the tombs. By the fallen pillars."

"Ah. Temple of Serqet."

"Serqet?"

The old man regarded the necklace with an odd mixture of reverence and trepidation. "Scorpion goddess. She who stops breath."

"You mean she was beautiful?" Tremayne asked. "Breathtaking?"

The elder's laugh was dry and cracked. "No. She steal breath from body. Men die."

"Oh, well, that's cheery," Harry muttered.

"Serqet has power over snakes and scorpions." The old man eyed the glistening pendant in Hester's lap as if expecting it to come alive. "She can protect from bite or send scorpion to punish. In the afterlife she gives breath of life to the deserving dead." He sent Hester a hard stare. "You see other signs of goddess?"

Hester frowned. "Well, we saw a snake. I threw a rock at it."

The old man nodded, apparently unsurprised. "Omen. Symbol of royalty."

Tremayne looked highly skeptical. "So this necklace is old? Valuable?"

The old man ignored him and regarded Hester with dark, serious eyes. "You put on?" He mimed placing it around his neck.

"Uh, yes. I did. Briefly. Why?"

His wrinkled brow became even more furrowed. The look he sent her was both sympathetic and grim. "Then curse begins," he whispered gravely.

A shiver of apprehension raised the hairs on the back of Hester's neck, but Tremayne couldn't contain his snort of disbelief.

"Curse? What curse?"

The old man glared at him. "Serqet's curse. It is written on the stele of Ranthor."

Harry raised his brows. "And what kind of curse is it? Does the wearer get the attributes of a scorpion? The ability to paralyze their victims? To pinch with deadly accuracy? Does she get a poisonous tail?" He turned to Hester. "You're not cursed. Except with a sharp tongue and a willful temper, and those you had already."

The old man frowned at his irreverence. "Serqet was a goddess scorned."

Harry gave a low laugh. "And 'Hell hath no fury,' eh? Oh, believe me, I have plenty of experience with feminine ire."

"Of course you do," Hester said irritably. "One wonders who the widows and opera singers of London are fighting over in your absence."

Harry chuckled. "They're pining for me already, I guarantee it. But I was thinking of Aunt Agatha, actually. That woman could make a fire-breathing dragon behave. Cross her at your peril."

The old man ignored their byplay and sent Hester a significant look. "Serqet was betrayed in love. Her bitterness and anger cursed that which you hold in your hands."

Hester glanced down at the necklace. The silver and gems seemed to glitter malevolently in the thin beams of sunlight that pierced the dark interior of the hut.

"Serqet's gift holds great power; the power to destroy. The French emperor, Bonaparte, he learned of this. When he came to Egypt fifteen years ago, his greatest desire was to find . . . that. He believed the power of Serqet would make his assault on Europe unstoppable. He sent men far and wide, to all the temples and tombs, to search. I was part of one such team, sent to translate. We had no luck."

The elder's face split into a toothless grin. "To think, during all this time, it was here, at my very door!" He shook his head with a wry chuckle but then became serious once more. "But such power comes at a price. All the evils in the world shall befall you now, unless the curse is broken."

Tremayne snorted. "Lady Morden doesn't need any help attracting disaster. She's a one-woman danger zone. Only a few hours ago, I had to rescue her from the bottom of a well—"

Hester sent him a quelling glare, and he wisely let the rest of his sentence taper off.

"How is the curse undone?" she asked urgently.

The old man's dark eyes twinkled. "Only a love stronger than the hate that fills it can undo the scorpion's curse. A sacrifice from a true heart."

Tremayne slapped his palms on his knees and rose. "True heart. Sacrifice. Got it." He caught Hester's upper arm and practically dragged her to her feet. "Lovely talking to you, sir, but we'd best be off. Lady Morden's keen to find her bodyguard, you know. Good day."

Hester sent the old man a weak smile of thanks as Tremayne bustled her out the door.

As soon as they were safely out of earshot, he said, "What a load of codswallop. You don't believe any of that curse nonsense, do you? All the evils of the world. Ha!" He squinted up at the sky.

"What are you doing?"

"Checking for imminent peril. A sandstorm, maybe. Or a bolt of lightning. If you've suddenly been endowed with even greater powers of destruction than usual, I believe I ought to take cover."

"You shouldn't mock," Hester scolded, tucking the necklace back into her skirts. "He clearly believes the curse is real."

Tremayne shook his head. "Ancient Egyptian goddesses? Curses thousands of years old? It beggars belief, as old Shakespeare would say." He started back down the hill towards camp then pointed at a procession of camels and riders that was entering the village. "It seems we have company."

Hester recognized the dark-haired Italian at the head of the group and gave an audible groan.

Harry peered at her. "Do you know him?"

"Unfortunately, yes. That's Bernardino Drovetti, a treasure hunter working for the French. The British Consul, Henry Salt, warned me about him. He and Salt are dreadful rivals, each one vying to get their hands on the most interesting artifacts. Drovetti's reputation is rather unsavory. He mistreats those who work on his archaeological digs. I wouldn't trust him any further than I could throw him."

They watched as the procession drew nearer. Drovetti wore a loose, pale linen jacket and a white shirt open at the throat, displaying an alarming amount of chest hair. His face was deeply tanned. He directed his camel toward them, dismounted, and raised his white hat in greeting. He bowed low over Hester's hand and ignored Harry completely.

"Signora Morden!" he beamed, showing gleaming white teeth. "I am overjoyed to have found you."

It took Hester a great deal of willpower not to whip her arm away when his lips touched her skin. She extracted her hand from his clammy grip. "I thought you were working over at Thebes, Mr. Drovetti?"

"I was, my dear. I was. But my good friend, Signor Salt, he send me to look for you. He hear of the death of your uncle and was most concerned that you were out here alone."

Hester sent him a polite smile. "That is very kind of you, sir, but unnecessary. I do not require protection. My uncle's body-guard, Suleiman—"

"Has abandoned you," Drovetti finished with dramatic relish. "Yes! The locals, they tell me of his desertion. Perhaps after the death of your uncle he did not want to work for a female? Or perhaps he is simply a coward."

Hester stiffened. "I am sure it is neither of those things. It is most unlike Suleiman to go anywhere without telling me. I am concerned."

Drovetti shrugged. "Forget him. Allow me to offer my protection back to Cairo."

Harry stepped forward, and Drovetti eyed him with instant dislike.

"She's not alone. She has me, a fellow Englishman. She doesn't need your assistance."

"And who might you be, sir?"

"Harry Tremayne. I'm a friend of the family."

The Italian gave a stiff, formal bow. "Bernardino Drovetti. Such a pleasure to meet a European in this land of infidels." His insincerity was almost comical.

The masculine hostility between the two men made Hester want to roll her eyes. Really, they were like two wild dogs, squaring off against one another, fighting over some scrap of meat. Which made *her* the scrap. That was hardly flattering.

Drovetti stepped back. "I must set up camp before dark. We shall speak again, signora Morden."

* * *

HARRY WATCHED THE NEWCOMER LEAVE. The man's black hair had been slicked back with some kind of oil or pomade. He looked like a greased weasel. Women probably found him desperately attractive, but there was something calculating about his black eyes. They glinted with cunning. Surely Hester wouldn't be taken in by such a poseur?

Harry had always been an excellent judge of character; the war had taught him how to size up a man quickly, how to discern who would be good to have at his side during a skirmish, and who would turn tail and run at the critical moment. Drovetti, he was sure, was the kind of man who would hide under a pile of bodies and play dead until the fighting stopped.

"I hope you're not fooled by that oily display," he said.

Hester laughed, and something inside him eased just a fraction. "Of course not. Come on. Let's have some dinner."

CHAPTER 7

*D*rovetti reappeared as the sun was setting in a blaze of red behind the mountains. Harry glared at him over the remains of the lamb he'd roasted over the fire, but the Italian didn't take the hint that he was unwelcome. He strode through the lengthening shadows straight to Hester, his expression curiously intent.

"I hear you had a lucky discovery in the sand?" he said without preamble. "A necklace of some antiquity. May I be permitted to see it?"

Harry stood and moved closer to Hester, but she remained seated by the fire, apparently unconcerned. She reached into her pocket. The scorpion glimmered enticingly in the firelight.

Drovetti let out a long, slow whistle and his eyes gleamed. "What a find!" he murmured. "Quite remarkable, my dear. Middle Kingdom, perhaps?" A muscle ticked in his jaw, and he seemed barely able to contain his excitement. "Such a thing would be the highlight of any serious collection. I will give you a thousand English pounds for it."

Hester shook her head.

"Two thousand," he said quickly.

Harry almost grinned at the mulish expression on her face. It was one he was intimately acquainted with; the lady had made up her mind.

"I'm afraid it's not for sale, Mr. Drovetti. For any price. I'm taking it to my friend, the Bey, to go in the new museum he's planning."

The Italian's face fell, but he seemed to accept the refusal with good grace. "Ah, well. A noble sentiment, my dear. But do tell me if you change your mind. I have a collector who would be most pleased to obtain it."

He sent Harry a suspicious look, as if warning him to be on his best behavior. Harry sent him a superior sneer in return.

"I bid you good night."

Harry let out a snort as soon as Drovetti had gone. "That was too easy. Did you see the look on his face? Pure avarice. He wants that necklace, and he'll do anything to get it, you mark my words. We need to be on guard."

Hester nodded. "I fear you're right. Still, forewarned is forearmed, as they say."

Harry sent her a smug glance. "Ready to admit how glad you are that I'm here?"

"Never. I can look after myself, thank you very much. I'm not such a ninny that I'm going to leave this lying around the place for him to steal." She lifted the necklace and refastened it around her neck. "There. He'll find it difficult to steal now."

She rose, slipped into her tent, and returned with a large linen bathing sheet. "I need to wash. All that scrambling around dusty tombs has left me filthy. I'm going to the oasis. You can stand watch so no one disturbs me."

She didn't wait for Harry's agreement. She simply headed off down the path toward the water. Harry swore under his breath. High-handed little minx. He wasn't her servant, forced to obey her every command.

And yet he scrambled after her.

At the water's edge he discovered a set of steps and a low wall had been built to allow easy access. He eyed the inky surface with misgiving. "Aren't you worried about crocodiles?"

"Don't be silly. There are no crocodiles in here. Only a few fish, and they're harmless enough. It's human interference I'm concerned about. I usually have Suleiman stand guard for me, but you'll have to do."

Hester slipped behind a large date palm and Harry heard the ominous rustle of clothing being removed. He experienced a flash of alarm. "You're not going *completely* in the water are you? I thought you just meant to wash your face."

"Of course I am." Her tone was impatient. "I need a bath. And, ruffian though you are, I trust you're enough of a gentleman to afford me some privacy and not peek."

Harry snorted. Her belief in his willpower was clearly stronger than his own. He was a healthy, red-blooded male. Did she really think he could stand with his back to the water the entire time, knowing she was naked or practically naked, right there next to him? Honestly, she would try the patience of a saint, and he certainly wasn't in that category.

"I bet your precious Suleiman peeks," he said.

More rustling. Harry tried very hard not to imagine which piece of clothing she was removing now. What was she wearing under that damned too-tight shirt that showed every gorgeous curve? A corset? Surely not; it was too hot for such things. Stays? He imagined her untying the ribbon at the shoulder. Slipping down the cotton of her shift to reveal a creamy expanse of skin. Beautiful, soft, sweet-smelling skin.

His brain went a little fuzzy, and he bit back a groan. He'd been without a woman for far too long.

"I doubt it," Hester said matter-of-factly, breaking into his erotic reverie. "The poor man's a eunuch. I suspect he's not particularly interested in seeing me, or any woman, naked."

Harry winced in sympathy even as he said, "He's still a man,

Hester. How can you be so naïve? A man will take *any* excuse to look at a naked woman, whether or not he's had his bollo—"

"Oh, hush!' she scolded. "Have you turned around?"

Harry exhaled a put-upon sigh. "Yes."

He heard scampering footsteps and then the splash of water as she entered the oasis. He crossed his arms over his chest and rolled his eyes upward, praying to whatever gods might be listening for patience.

Clearly the powers that be had decided to punish him by placing a pithy, prickly termagant in his life. And then they'd exacerbated the aggravation by making him want her. He'd prayed his infatuation would fade over time, but the feeling hadn't abated. If anything, it had grown worse. He'd lusted and despaired over Lady Hester Morden in equal measure for years.

It was almost completely dark now, the shadows deep purple and indigo. But an impossibly large moon and a smattering of stars silvered everything in a pale halo, and Harry ground his teeth and tried not to think of the way the moonbeams would highlight her cheek, her arms, the luscious curve of her breasts.

He'd never seen her naked, of course, but he'd imagined it a thousand times. Water droplets would chase each other over her peaked nipples and down the long slope of her spine. He imagined his tongue following those droplets, licking the wetness from her skin...

His breeches had become uncomfortably tight. He readjusted himself and refused to look. He was no voyeur. No randy youth. He was Orpheus; Eurydice would be dragged back to the underworld if he so much as glanced around. He clenched his fists against temptation.

This, surely, was the most exquisite torture ever devised. If he hadn't shown himself a bloody hero during the war—and he had a drawerful of medals back home to prove it—then he'd definitely done so now. Hester was like the oasis: a welcome miracle, refreshing and beautiful. And he was parched for a taste of her.

At long last, he heard her leave the water and duck back behind the tree to dress.

"Would you like to bathe?" she asked. "I promise not to look." There was a teasing laugh in her voice that made him want to throttle her.

He should call her bluff. She'd probably never seen a naked man before. He could just imagine her shock at seeing him in all his fully-aroused glory. She'd probably faint. Then again, Hester never did what was expected. She'd probably just look at him curiously and demand what was the matter with him. Wouldn't that be interesting?

"I'll do it later," he ground out.

They'd almost reached the tent, with her complaining about her wet hair, when he stopped in his tracks and ducked down.

"Shh!"

"Don't you shhh me, you overgrown—"

"Be quiet!" he hissed.

He glanced sideways at her. Her mouth had stalled in a perfect O, and her eyes widened as she finally noticed what he had: the shadowy figure sneaking around the outside of her tent.

He tugged her behind a cluster of date palms.

"It's Drovetti!" she whispered indignantly. "Why, that sneaky devil! He's trying to steal my necklace!"

She put her hand up to it, still fastened around her neck, and Harry wondered if she'd taken it off to bathe. The mental image that flashed into his brain—Hester, naked in the moonlight save for the strange, otherworldly necklace, like some irresistible Egyptian goddess—made his blood pound in his temples.

Thankfully, she didn't notice his inattention. She scowled as Drovetti ducked under the tent flap and went inside. "The fiend! Well, he won't find anything in there."

Drovetti clearly came to the same conclusion. After a few minutes he reappeared and slunk off into the shadows.

"I doubt he'll be back tonight," Harry said, "but just to be on the safe side, I'll sleep there." He pointed to a spot in front of her tent, then went to his saddlebag and withdrew his bedroll. Hester, to his surprise, didn't argue.

"Thank you," she said. "I would appreciate that." She ducked inside her tent then almost immediately stuck her head back out again. "Oh, don't forget to put your socks over the top of your boots. It stops the snakes and scorpions getting in. Goodnight."

*I*t took Hester a long time to get to sleep. She was far too aware of Tremayne sleeping less than three feet away from her, albeit on the other side of the material. She tensed every time she heard him sigh, sniff, or turn over.

In truth, she was rather disappointed that he hadn't turned round even once while she was bathing. She hadn't been brave enough to go completely naked; she'd kept her shift on in the water, but she'd assumed an unrepentant rogue like him would have at least tried to steal a glance.

Was she really so unattractive? Harry said men always wanted to see naked women, but he'd been all too able to resist the temptation of seeing her, hadn't he?

Hester sighed and punched her pillow. Not that she *wanted* him to look at her. Still, it would be nice to be thought of as an attractive woman for once, instead of an annoying, over-educated harridan.

The sun had barely risen when she was awakened by one of the local boys talking urgently to Harry. She pulled on a shirt and her split skirts and emerged from the tent.

"Are you sure?" Harry asked.

The boy nodded vehemently. "Yes. It is the lady's man, Suleiman, calling for help. I hear him."

"Where?" Hester demanded.

The boy pointed to the remains of the Roman fort at the opposite end of the oasis. "There. His voice comes from the ground."

Hester glanced at Harry. "There are several chambers below ground and tunnels to direct the water. He could have fallen into one of those."

Tremayne nodded grimly. "All right, let's go."

He rose, and Hester saw him withdraw two pistols from beneath his bedroll, check them, and stuff them into the waistband of his breeches at the back. He shrugged into his jacket, tugged on his boots, slung his leather satchel across his body, and set off in the direction the boy had indicated.

Hester pulled on her own stockings and ankle boots—after checking them for scorpions—and hurried after him. She was out of breath by the time she caught up with him. His long legs seemed to eat up the ground and she had to hurry to keep pace.

"Suleiman?" she shouted as they neared the ruins. They stopped and listened and were rewarded by a faint moan. "Over there. He sounds hurt."

They clambered over a waist-high wall and rounded a corner, but the figure they encountered was not Suleiman. It was Drovetti.

Hester heard Harry curse. He stepped in front of her, shielding her with his body, but not before she caught sight of the wicked-looking pistol the Italian had leveled at Harry's chest.

"Good morning!" Drovetti said cheerfully. "I regret to do this to you, my dear, but I must insist that you give me that necklace. Emperor Bonaparte has been seeking it for a long time, you see, ever since he became aware of the legend. He is sure it is his destiny."

"Napoleon's safely locked up on Elba," Harry said coolly. "I fought for two years to make sure of it."

Drovetti smiled. "You haven't heard the news? The emperor has escaped his island prison. Even now he marches toward Paris to rally his faithful troops. With the power of Serqet, all Europe will bow to his glory. He will be exceedingly grateful—and generous—to the man who brings it to him."

Hester took a step forward and placed her hand on Harry's back. His muscles jumped at her touch, and he tensed as she slid her hand down and wrapped her fingers around the butt of one of the pistols.

"Don't do it," he said slowly. He shook his head in a vehement denial, but whether it was directed at herself or Drovetti, Hester didn't know.

Drovetti chuckled with almost childlike glee, and Hester realized with a start that he was quite mad.

"Oh, I'm afraid I must," he said cheerfully. "Signora Morden, please do not try to use the pistols Tremayne has behind his back. I will not hesitate to shoot him. And you," he added softly, "if you do not do exactly as I say. Now, I want you to pull them out and place them on the ground. Slowly."

With a sigh of defeat, Hester did as she was told. She placed the pistols in the dirt then straightened to stand beside Tremayne. He tried to shove her behind him again, but she held her ground. She would not let him take a bullet meant for her.

"Perfect." Drovetti smiled approvingly. He motioned with the barrel of the pistol toward her throat. "Now. The necklace."

Anger heated her blood as Hester began to unfasten the chain. To her distress, it was a struggle to release the clasp, but then, suddenly, it came free. "You are nothing but a common thief," she said scathingly. "A cheat and a blackguard."

Drovetti gave an elegant shrug. "I've been called far worse. Now, toss the necklace to me."

Hester was tempted to hurl it at his head, but she was too

afraid of him firing the pistol and hitting Tremayne. She threw it in a graceful arc and Drovetti caught it neatly in his free hand. It disappeared into the inner pocket of his coat.

He motioned them back toward a doorway in the wall, set with an open iron gate. "Down there, if you please."

Stone steps descended into darkness, and Hester shuddered but complied. Harry followed, backing away from Drovetti until they were both several feet lower than him. The Italian smiled as he closed the gate and secured it with a padlock.

"See how noble I am," he said. "I'm not even going to shoot you. Someone from the village will miss you eventually and come looking—although not before I'm far away from here. I paid that young lad handsomely to forget he'd seen you. It might be a day or two before you're missed." He chuckled and tipped his hat. "Addio."

Tremayne leapt toward the gate and rattled the bars as soon as Drovetti's footfalls faded, but to no avail; the metal was firmly implanted in the stone, and the wall was in an unusually good state of repair. There wasn't even space to climb up over it or squeeze beneath it. With a sigh of frustration, he turned and sat on the top step and rested his elbows on his knees. "Bugger."

Hester silently agreed. "Do you really think Napoleon believes in the power of the necklace?"

Harry shrugged. "I don't know. Even if there's no truth to the legend, there's power in *believing* in something. If Bonaparte's convinced it's his destiny to win, it'll give him an edge. Confidence can make all the difference in a battle." He raked a hand through his hair. "Bloody hell. I hope Drovetti was lying about his escape. I've wasted two years of my life at war. I'm sick to death of it."

Hester glanced uncertainly down the steps. "Where do you think that goes?"

Harry opened his satchel and withdrew the tinder box and a

candle. "We might as well find out. There's no getting out this way."

The steps descended belowground and turned into a cavern-like cellar of impressive size, the lower part of which was filled with clear turquoise water. A small amount of light filtered in from somewhere below, sending undulating reflections across Tremayne's handsome features.

Hester glanced around in interest. "This must be some sort of cistern." Her voice echoed around the vaulted arches of the ceiling. "The Romans built a whole series of underground aqueducts around here to channel water for irrigation."

Tremayne sent her an amused glance. "You seem to be spending quite a bit of time in wells and watercourses this week, Lady Morden. Look on the bright side; at least you're not trapped down here alone. You have the pleasure of my charming company." He looked around, holding the candle aloft. "It's rather picturesque."

"It is not *picturesque*. It is wet. And dank. And probably rat-infested."

"Oh, come. Look at those lovely gothic arches." Tremayne wiggled his eyebrows. "Here we have a barrel vault." He pointed out over the water. "And that, there, with a cross in the center, is a groin vault."

"I don't care what kind of vault it is," Hester said irritably. "If it rains, we shall likely be drowned."

"You said it never rains here," he reminded her. "If it does, you'll have to kiss me."

She shook her head then frowned as he handed her the candle, sat down, and started pulling off his boots. "What are you doing?"

"There's an entrance down there. Under the water. I'm going to see if it's a way out." He placed his satchel aside and stripped off his jacket. For one breathless moment she wondered if he was going to remove his shirt, too, but he clearly decided against it, and she experienced an irrational moment of pique. He lowered himself into the clear water, swam forward a few strokes, and then dived under the surface.

Hester held her breath as she watched him swim towards the lighter section. It seemed to be extremely far down. She let out a moan of dismay as he disappeared completely. Good lord, where had he gone? Was he drowning down there? Had he abandoned her?

Tense moments later her heart almost burst with relief when he reappeared. His head broke the surface, and he took a deep lungful of air. "It's an exit, all right." He grinned, treading water. "But it's quite far down. How well can you swim?"

"Tolerably well. But I'm not sure I can hold my breath for as long as you can."

He pulled himself out onto the side next to her, like a dripping merman. His shirt was almost transparent. It sucked and molded to his chest and arms with distracting precision, and Hester glanced away, suddenly hot.

"You can do it," he cajoled. "I'll guide you."

She shook her head. "Why don't *you* swim through, go back to the village, and come back with a way to open the gate? I'll stay right here and wait for you."

"No time for that. I'll be damned if I let Drovetti get away with stealing our necklace."

"*My* necklace."

"Oh, all right, *your* necklace. We need to get after him as soon as possible."

Hester couldn't fault the logic of that. "Oh, very well."

She followed Tremayne back up the steps and watched as he pushed his boots, satchel, and jacket out between the bars of the gate. He turned and sent her an expectant look. "What are you waiting for? You can't swim in those skirts. Take 'em off."

Hester glared at him. He was correct, of course; the extra fabric would become waterlogged and make swimming impossible, but the thought of undressing down to her shift and stays in front of him was mortifying.

He reached out to unlace the front tie of her shirt, but she batted his hands away. "I can manage without assistance, thank you!"

He shrugged and sent her a wicked grin. "Just trying to be helpful."

He went back down the steps, presumably to give her a little privacy, and with a growl of resignation, she made short work of stepping out of her split skirts and shirt. Warm air swirled around her bare legs, exposed to the knee by her short cotton shift, and she glanced down in despair at the ridiculously feminine item.

Before she'd come to Egypt she'd purchased the most beautiful French undergarments—sheer as gossamer and trimmed with lace. She'd told herself it was practical, because of the heat, but she'd always experienced a deliciously feminine thrill whenever she pulled the material over her skin. She'd never thought anyone would actually *see* her in them.

Now, as the sun heated the bare skin on her shoulders and the curve of her breasts above her short stays, she realized how very immodest they were. Still, Harry Tremayne probably wouldn't even bat an eyelid. He'd doubtless seen far more attractive women in far less.

Hester descended the stairs. As expected, Tremayne only spared her a brief glance before he looked away. He was already back in the water, and she lowered herself down next to him with a little shiver at the cooler temperature. Her shift ballooned up around her waist, and she shoved it back down to protect her modesty.

He glanced round at her, his eyes sparkling with mischief. "Ready for an adventure? There's an arched tunnel down there, very short, with an iron grate like a portcullis. You need to swim beneath it—there's a gap of about two feet. Just follow me."

Hester nodded. Her heart was already beating urgently against her ribs. Tremayne took a deep breath and dived below the surface, and Hester did the same.

The water was incredibly clear. Kicking her legs, she followed him down toward the patch of light. Her ears popped. He disappeared under the stone archway, and she saw him wriggle his way beneath the metal grill he'd described. Once he was through, he turned in the water and beckoned her forward, extending his hand.

Her lungs were beginning to burn. She caught hold of the metal spikes and started to swim beneath them, but her back scraped on the jagged metal, and she felt the material of her stays catch—and hold. An involuntary moan escaped her mouth, and she expelled a surprised batch of bubbles.

She opened her eyes wide and started to thrash wildly. Oh, god, she was stuck and running out of air. Never had she wanted to suck in a breath more, but there was water, water everywhere and she would drown if she inhaled.

And then, suddenly, Harry was there. His palms cupped her cheeks, holding her head still as his eyes met hers through the clear water. He looked calm, determined. Capable. Before she could fathom what he meant to do, he tilted his head and sealed his mouth over hers.

Her lips parted in surprise, and to her amazement she felt him *breathe* into her mouth, pushing air into her lungs. It was a most peculiar feeling. She inhaled what he exhaled, and the unbearable tightness in her chest eased.

The world steadied. Harry withdrew his mouth, sent her a satisfied nod, then reached behind her and tugged at her stays. They came free with a sudden jolt, and he grabbed her hand and kicked his legs, propelling them both to the surface.

They emerged with great gasping breaths, sucking air into their lungs. Harry let out a wild whooping cry of triumph, and Hester began to laugh, gasping and spluttering in disbelief.

They were only twenty feet from the bank. They hauled themselves out of the water onto the sandy beach and collapsed, panting, on their backs beneath the swaying date palms. Hester's chest was rising and falling rapidly, and she rolled her head to the side to find Tremayne in no better condition. A grin split his face as he looked back at her.

"That does *not* count as a kiss," she rasped unsteadily.

He chuckled, then coughed, then laughed again. "Your face! I've never seen a woman so surprised. And of course it doesn't count as a kiss. When I kiss a woman I don't want her thinking she's about to die. Unless it's from pleasure, of course."

The look he sent her was pure wickedness, and Hester felt a flush suffuse her entire body. She belatedly recalled that she was only wearing her shift and stays. A shift that, like Tremayne's shirt, had presumably been rendered practically transparent.

A glance down her body revealed her worst fears. Her legs, stomach, and even the valley between her thighs were clearly visible. She sat up with a gasp and plastered her hands over her breasts.

Tremayne chuckled again at her mortification and clambered to his feet then offered her a hand up, which she ignored.

"Come on, Morden. It's not as if I haven't seen a naked female before. I swear I'm not about to molest you. Let's go get our clothes."

hen they returned to the village, it was to discover that Drovetti had indeed already left. The locals reported him taking the trail back toward Alexandria.

Harry followed Hester into her tent and stopped dead, staring aghast at her belongings. "Good God. How much luggage do you need, woman?" He strode to a packing chest containing her portable medicine kit and writing slope and shook his head. "How long will it take you to pack all this up?"

"A few hours, perhaps? I usually have Suleiman to help me."

Harry groaned. "I don't suppose you'd consider leaving it and—"

"You suppose correctly. I'm not going anywhere without my maps, or my clothes, or any of my belongings. Those charts are Uncle Jasper's life's work. I'm not simply—"

"Drovetti already has a good hour's head start on us. We don't stand a chance of catching him unless we leave right now."

"Yes, we do."

Harry raised a skeptical brow. "Oh really? How?"

"We can take a short cut."

Harry sank down onto the edge of her cot and ran his fingers through his hair. "A short cut," he repeated dryly.

Hester rummaged through the pile of papers on her desk and found the one she sought. "Yes. Drovetti's following the old trade route through the desert. It's not very direct. It meanders back and forth, keeping to lower ground."

She unrolled her map and beckoned him forward, pointing with her finger. "Uncle Jasper and I charted several Berber caravan routes which cut through the hills. If we take one of them, it will considerably shorten our journey. We can catch up with Drovetti and steal the necklace back before he reaches Alexandria."

Tremayne stared down at the paper and nodded slowly. "And you're certain this is accurate enough not to get us lost? The maps we used in the army were always promising shortcuts to somewhere or other, and what looked like a nice mountain path usually ended up being an impassable goat track or a rocky stream instead."

Hester shot him an offended look. "Of course I'm certain. This is the most up-to-date map ever produced of the region."

Harry gave a resigned sigh. "All right, then. Let's get packing."

In the end, it took them less than an hour to stow everything away. Tremayne proved astonishingly efficient. Hester spoke to one of the locals and arranged for the larger, nonessential items such as her campaign desk, writing slope, portmanteau, tea set, rugs, and several trunks of clothes to be conveyed to the home of Sir Henry Salt, the British Consul in Cairo.

She retained only a single change of clothes, Uncle Jasper's charts, and her medicine kit, which she secured neatly in saddle-bags on the back of her mount.

Tremayne eyed the animal with intense dislike.

"A camel? Must you be so eccentric? What's wrong with a horse, for goodness sake?"

Hester patted Bahaba's wooly cheek. He had ridiculously long eyelashes, like a girl.

"This is Bahaba. He's incredibly stubborn and impossible to control, but despite his irritable nature, I'm quite fond of him. He's dependable. And he's not a camel. He's a dromedary. He has one hump, see. Camels have two."

Harry patted the arched neck of his horse, and the animal tossed its head proudly and shivered under the caress. Its dark coat had a velvety sheen in the sunlight, and its muscles twitched with restrained impatience. Hester had to admit that the animal was a great deal more attractive than smelly old Bahaba.

"This is Makeen," Harry said, his voice soft with pride. "I'm told that means 'strong'. He's an Arabian: intelligent, spirited, fast as the wind." He scratched the horse on its forehead, between its large, liquid eyes, and the animal snickered in delight. "I bought him in Alexandria, and I don't think I can bear to sell him again. I'm going to have to find a way to get you back to England, aren't I, my handsome boy?"

Hester's own body prickled in awareness as she imagined Harry's strong, sensitive hands stroking *her* the way he caressed the horse.

She forced herself to exhale. "The Bedouins certainly appreciate fine horseflesh. They have a saying: 'My treasures do not chink or glitter. They gleam in the sun and neigh in the night.' And when they gift a horse to someone, they say, 'I give thee flight without wings.'"

Harry's smile made her heart miss a beat. "I like that. Flight without wings. That's very apt."

He mounted in one swift, easy movement, a move he'd obviously perfected over a thousand instances in the Horse Guards, and they set off.

* * *

THEY LAPSED into a companionable silence as Hester led them out of the village and found a barely-discernible trail that led off into the hills. Harry would have thought it was nothing more than a goat track, but she seemed confident of their bearings, and he had enough confidence in her abilities to allow her to lead.

For now.

After a while she glanced sideways at him. "You ride very well."

Harry fought not to smile at the grudging compliment.

"You were in the Horse Guards, were you not?" she prodded.

"Yes. I love horses, so it made sense to join a cavalry regiment. It was a stupid mistake, in hindsight. I hated seeing them killed."

Harry frowned, amazed that he'd said such a thing. He never would have admitted to such a weakness back in London, but Hester was so easy to talk to, and they were in the middle of nowhere. Maintaining a stiff upper lip seemed rather pointless.

He shrugged. "I learned not to get too attached to them. It was less painful when I lost one, that way. Some died of battle wounds, others from not enough to eat." He stared straight ahead, concentrating on the stony trail they were following.

"I had a horse shot out from under me at Badajoz. It fell and pinned me, and I couldn't escape. The French came to finish off the wounded, but I was saved by darkness falling. I managed to crawl back to my own line."

He noticed the look of pity and concern on her face and sent her an easy smile to lighten the tone. "You, too, ride very well. Although I can't quite picture you riding that monstrous beast down Rotten Row. You'd give the ladies of the *ton* heart palpitations."

He smiled when she snorted in amusement.

"I'm not sure my reputation would recover from the scandal. An unattached heiress can be forgiven a great deal, but riding a dromedary in Hyde Park might be taking it too far." She sighed, as if the thought of being back in London depressed her. "I suppose I could always learn to drive a curricle and pair. I do enjoy acquiring new skills."

Harry glanced at her profile, at the lush perfection of her lips, and his mind—naturally—wondered whether she'd extend that enthusiasm to learning new sexual experiences. God, the things he could show her.

Her fair skin had been caressed by the sun's rays, and he found her freckles ridiculously attractive. He wanted to lick them, like cinnamon sprinkles on an iced bun. In London she would be decried as a sun-browned heathen, but compared to the semi-transparent watery misses of the *ton*, whose skin was so pale you could see their blue veins beneath their sallow skin, Hester was a vibrant, sun-kissed goddess.

Why should the sun be the only one to kiss her? Harry's eyes roved the curve of her jaw, the straight line of her nose. Was she that beautiful peachy color all over? Or did she have paler areas on the places that seldom saw the sun?

He readjusted his position in the saddle.

"Napoleon was a dreadful rider, by all accounts," he said, to give himself something to think about other than his hands on her skin. His voice held a telltale roughness, but he hoped she'd ascribe that to a parched throat, rather than to a terminal case of lust. He patted Makeen's neck. "He had an Arabian too, a grey named Marengo."

"You saw him?"

"A few times, but only from afar. He slouched in the saddle and never kept his heels down. Rumor has it he was always falling off."

Hester frowned. "Perhaps if Drovetti gives him the necklace, he'll be able to ride as well as—" she stopped suddenly, and Harry had the distinct impression she'd been about to say 'as well as you' but then decided she didn't want to flatter him and amended it to, "—as if he was born in the saddle."

They entered a rugged gorge and started following a rocky

riverbed in a vaguely southerly direction. Harry glanced upwards at the towering hundred-foot cliffs that rose on either side. It was starkly beautiful. They hadn't seen another living creature for the past hour, save a few goats, but at least it was shady.

A couple of birds of prey that looked rather like vultures drifted lazily in the warm air currents above them, and he wondered if they were some kind of ill omen. They reminded him of the fortune hunters back in London, making a tour of the ballroom, circling toward their prey.

Hester, with her fortune, had always been in their sights. He'd had a hard time of it, steering them clear of her without her noticing his interference. He hadn't wanted her hurt, trapped into a marriage with someone who only wanted her money and couldn't appreciate the vibrant, headstrong woman he knew her to be.

After another mile or so, she pulled her mount to a halt and unrolled her precious map. She squinted out at the horizon then back down. "Not far now."

Harry couldn't resist teasing her. "Admit it. We're lost."

She rose perfectly to the bait. Her cheeks flushed pink, and her eyes flashed with temper.

"We are not lost."

"Are you saying mapmakers *never* get lost?" he pressed. "I find that very hard to believe."

She sent him an exasperated glance. "Everyone gets lost at some point in their lives, Tremayne. But I usually don't get lost *again*." She tilted her head and then sent him a smile that made his heart thud heavily in his chest. "Actually, there's something quite nice about getting lost sometimes. One finds all manner of exciting things." She waved the parchment at him. "After all, what is a map if not the potential for adventure, a chance to discover new worlds? It is freedom."

He decided to argue, just to be contrary. "A map is a *lie*. Think about it. Every map is subjective; you select what to put on it.

Only the information that is essential to fulfill its particular purpose is included—here in relation to there. It doesn't tell the whole story. It is the world reduced to points, lines, and textures." He shook his head, as if he found her view of the world woefully lacking.

As expected, she glared at him as if he'd just kicked a kitten. He bit back a smile. What he wouldn't give to have all that righteous fury in his arms, in his bed. He cleared his throat and sent her a smile sure to irritate.

"There's nothing for it," she said. "I shall have to strangle you."

He bit back a laugh. "Oh, you will, will you? And how do you propose to do that? I'm bigger than you. And stronger. And far more versed in hand-to-hand combat."

She sent him a serene smile. "Oh, where there's a will there's a way, Tremayne. The gods of poetic justice will surely grant me victory."

Harry decided he'd be a fool not to check his socks for scorpions and his coffee for arsenic when they stopped to make camp. He wouldn't put it past her to poison him, the ungrateful wench.

It was just as well she had no idea of the power she held over him. He'd probably *let* her strangle him, if only to feel those hands on his skin. It would be the work of a moment to hook his legs behind her ankles and sweep her feet from under her. She'd fall to the ground—he'd cushion her fall with his body, of course —and then she'd be in his arms, with those glorious curves he'd glimpsed beneath her wet undergarments pressed against him—

She clicked her tongue and said something in Arabic. The dromedary, Bahaba, sank to the ground, folding its legs beneath it with a deep grumble of annoyance. She dismounted with far more grace than Harry imagined he would manage in the circumstances. He fanned himself with his hat and tried to cool his errant thoughts.

"If my estimations are correct," she said, "which I assure you they *are*, then we should catch up with Drovetti first thing in the morning. It will soon be too dark to continue, however, so I suggest we camp here for the night." She raised her brows at him in blatant challenge. "Unless you have any objection?"

Harry shook his head and kicked his boot out of the stirrup. "No objection at all, Lady Morden. I bow to your superior knowledge of the terrain."

She sent him a suspicious look, as if she couldn't decide whether he was being sarcastic or not, but she decided not to argue. Many men of his acquaintance would have been loath to let a woman take charge, in any situation, but he spoke nothing less than the truth. Not only did he trust her competence, he found it irresistibly attractive.

CHAPTER 10

*H*ester couldn't stop herself from sneaking glances at Harry across the fire, even though she tried not to. With a spurt of self-directed irritation, she picked up a handful of pebbles and tossed them, one by one, towards a larger stone she'd designated as a target.

She was restless and impatient, and she didn't know why. No, that was a lie: she *did* know why. It was the presence of the man sprawled on a blanket across the fire from her, stretched out on his side like a sated Roman senator, his elbow resting on his saddle, his long, lean body relaxed and yet still curiously alert in the flickering shadows.

They'd pitched her tent on one side of the rocky gorge and eaten a selection of cold foods she'd brought from the oasis. Olives and dates, figs and honey. The Ancient Egyptians had eaten the same in honor of Ma'at, the goddess of truth and balance, to remind themselves that the truth is sweet.

Hester forced herself to be truthful. Watching Harry eat had been an exercise in self-restraint. Her eyes had been constantly drawn to his tanned fingers, to his mobile lips as he placed a morsel into his mouth. The fascinating muscles that flexed at the side of his jaw as he chewed. The sinews of his forearm as he took a sip of water from his pouch.

What was wrong with her? She'd found the man attractive before, in the formal eveningwear of London's ballrooms. He was devastating in a black jacket and white cravat. But she found him even more attractive here, beneath the milky starlight, ruffled, unbuttoned, and sexily disheveled. Her fingers itched to touch the hint of beard that had appeared on his cheeks. Would it be soft, or prickly?

The remnant of a poem told to her by one of the Bey's wives flitted through her brain, an echo from some ancient text or other.

MAN OF MY HEART, *my beloved man,*
  your allure is a sweet thing, as sweet as honey.
  You have captivated me,
  of my own free will I will come to you.

HESTER THREW ANOTHER STONE. She was pathetic. Yearning for a man who didn't want her. He might have offered to marry her two years ago back in London, but that had only been because society expected it of him. He'd acted recklessly, kissing her at that fete, and as tempting as it had been to say yes, she'd known that only heartbreak could come from such a rashly issued proposal.

He would have come to resent her, to hate her for trapping him in a loveless—or, at least, one-sided—marriage. He didn't love her. He might find her amusing and a tolerable, if eccentric, companion, but he certainly didn't cherish any deeper feelings for her.

She was a realist. She'd seen plenty of examples of marriages of convenience in the *ton*. An arrangement like that was not for her. It would have broken her heart to watch Harry take a mistress mere months after the wedding.

If only he weren't the embodiment of her ideal man.

She'd been aware of him beside her all day, sure and effortless in the saddle. He never tried to rule his mount with brute strength, but urged it onward with masterful control like the Berber tribesmen of the desert. The sight of his hands on the leather reins made her stomach give a funny little flip.

It was impossible not to notice the way his breeches outlined his narrow hips and thighs, the hard ridges of his muscles clearly visible through the fabric. He was so vital, so exhilarating. Just being near him caused her heart to catch in her throat.

This was what she'd been missing, she realized. Uncle Jasper had been a wonderful traveling companion, but she'd been lonely without someone her own age. She'd missed Harry and his easy banter, his lazy smiles and his infuriating teasing. She felt more alive when he was in the vicinity.

Her spirits drooped. For months now she'd had a niggling sense of dissatisfaction, a feeling that she was searching for something elusive that kept evading her, no matter where she looked, how far she traveled.

She tossed the last stone and missed the rock. She'd be expected to marry when she got back to England. Was it too unrealistic to expect friendship, security, even love from a marriage? A partner with whom to have adventures, not someone who would barely tolerate her presence?

Impatient with herself, Hester stood and searched for more pebbles. It was hard to see the ground beyond the warm glow of firelight, but she persevered. She'd just collected a suitable handful when she felt a sharp stabbing sensation in her ankle, just above the protection of her boot.

"Ouch!"

She leapt sideways and caught a flash of movement as a scorpion scuttled under a nearby rock.

"Damn and blast. I've been stung!"

She scowled, furious at herself for not paying closer attention. She half hopped, half hobbled back to her rug by the fire. "Owww, it hurts!"

Tremayne had jumped to his feet at her shout and rushed forward to help her sit.

"What was it? A snake?"

"A scorpion," she gasped, hastening to unlace her boot. "I need to remove this before my foot starts to swell."

With an impatient sound he pushed aside her fumbling fingers , cut through the laces of her boot, and yanked it off.

"What kind of scorpion?" he urged. "Did you see it? Was it black or brown? Someone told me that the dark ones are less poisonous than the light-colored ones."

Hester winced against the pain. "It was hard to see in the darkness. But I think it was the dark kind."

He bent and took hold of her ankle, pushing up her skirts to expose her stockinged leg.

"A scorpion sting is rarely fatal for an adult, Tremayne," she said breathlessly. "It just hurts. Like a bee sting. Or a hot needle in my leg." She tried to push her skirts back down, but he ignored her struggles.

"Don't be missish, Hester. I've encountered scorpion stings before. A fellow in my regiment was stung in Portugal. We need to extract the poison. Take off your stocking, and I'll suck it out."

"You'll do no such thing!" The flush that seared her cheeks was nothing to do with the effects of the sting and everything to do with the thought of Harry Tremayne's mouth on any part of her—even somewhere as innocuous as an ankle. "There's a medicine kit in my saddle bag. Get that."

Harry shot her a look of pure frustration but went to do as she commanded. He rummaged around in her leather satchel and withdrew the box of medicines.

"You look very pale." A frown creased his forehead as he

opened the leather case. "God, these all look the same." He squinted at the small bottles. "I can barely read the labels."

Hester managed a weak smile. "Uncle Jasper's handwriting was never very legible. Look for the one called 'Brown's Linctus.' It's a tincture of Laudanum. It should relieve the pain a little."

Harry angled the bottles toward the firelight, selected one, and unstoppered the cork. Hester took a deep swig and sank back against her bedroll with a sigh.

The pain in her calf was a sharp throb, and she felt nauseous and shaky. She sucked in a deep breath. Thankfully, the tincture began to work almost immediately. A wonderful feeling of calm washed over her, and the pain lessened considerably. She became warm and languid, almost drowsy.

Hester frowned. She'd taken this medicine before, when she'd fallen from Bahaba and bruised her bottom. She didn't recall feeling quite so . . . relaxed. She lifted the bottle Harry had given her and tried to decipher Uncle Jasper's execrable scrawl.

"Oh dear."

Tremayne glanced at her sharply. "What is it? What's the matter?" He placed his palm on her forehead and pushed her hair back from her face.

His features swam in her vision. Hester waved the bottle in his direction and tried to summon up a proper sense of outrage. "Tremayne, you great idiot! You've given me the wrong one!"

CHAPTER 11

*H*arry frowned down at Hester in alarm. "What do you mean, the wrong one?" He grabbed the bottle from her unresisting grip. "'Brown's Linctus,' you said."

"Exactly! That's Blue Nile Lily!"

He sat back on his haunches. "Oh, hell. What does Blue Nile Lily do?"

"The Bey's doctor gave it to Uncle Jasper. He said it was primarily a painkiller—"

Harry expelled a relieved breath. "That's good then—"

"It's definitely working. My ankle doesn't hurt so much now." Her eyelids started to droop.

"You're not fainting are you? I can't stand women who faint."

She let out a soft laugh. "No. I'm fine. Just sleepy."

Her voice had taken on a dreamy quality, slightly slurred, as if she'd been drinking. Harry frowned. "Well, then. No harm done."

"Unless I experience the other effects the doctor mentioned," she murmured.

A fresh jolt of alarm hit him. "What other effects?"

She waved her hand in front of her face and almost swatted herself on the nose. "It's nothing. Really."

67

Harry squinted down at her. Her cheeks had turned a delicious shade of pink. "Are you blushing, Morden?"

"Of course not."

"What other effects?"

She let out a huff and rolled her eyes. "Like becoming. . . amorous."

His brows rose to his hairline. "You mean it's a *love potion?*" He tried to squash his crow of laughter and failed. "I've given you Uncle Jasper's love potion? Oh, that is priceless."

She turned her face away but he caught her chin and forced her gaze back to his. Her pupils were dark pools, almost drowning out the color of her irises.

"Look at me, Hester. Are you feeling amorous towards me?"

She batted his hand away and glared at him. "Stop teasing. It won't work on me. I don't even like you."

He chuckled, but she continued to look at him, studying his face with sudden intensity. And then she reached up and traced the line of his jaw, trailing her fingers from his ear to his chin and up over his lips.

Harry was too stunned to move. She'd never willingly touched him, ever, but the potion seemed to have loosened her inhibitions. Her caress left a tingling sensation in its wake.

"You *are* extremely handsome," she murmured. "I'll give you that."

"Uhm, thank you?" he said faintly.

"The ladies in the harem would be sighing all over you."

Before he could come up with a suitable answer to that, a frown marred her smooth forehead.

"I'm surprised you haven't tried to get rid of me by selling me to the nearest harem."

He fought to keep his tone light, even though her touch was doing funny things to his insides. "Believe me, I've been tempted."

She seemed to have forgotten that she was touching him—she was playing with a curl of hair by his ear now—but he was acutely aware of her touch. His body hardened to the point of pain. He cleared his throat.

"I doubt anyone would have you. Even if I offered to throw in a couple of camels and a nice Hamadan rug. Too much trouble, they'd say. And, by God, they'd be right."

She wrinkled her nose at him. "In some places," she said with a touch of asperity, "here being one of them, I am considered exotic. My pale skin and brown hair are a novelty." She pointed at the bridge of her nose, almost poking herself in the eye in the process. The potion had clearly affected her co-ordination.

"They've never seen freckles like this before. In England I might be scorned and left at the edge of the ballroom, but here, why, I bet some desert sheikh would pay handsomely to have me grace his tent."

She sounded so indignant that Harry had to smile, and yet the thought of another man with his hands on her—any man other than himself—made his blood seethe. An image of her pale limbs entwined with his on silken sheets flashed into his brain and he bit the inside of his cheek.

Good God, had no-one ever told her she was beautiful? The men in England were all blind. Or idiots. They were too used to pale, blue-eyed chits to appreciate the beauty of this one. Skin sprinkled with gold dust. Hair in glorious disarray. He'd always loved her hair; it was sinfully luxuriant, with hints of copper and bronze and paler streaks at the front, gilded by the sun. She was perverse, unusual, unforgettable.

Harry gazed down at her, almost lightheaded with desire. She was uncharted territory, a wonderful, infuriating mystery. He wanted to know every inch of her. To explore every valley and undulation.

Without thinking, he stroked her cheek, and she turned into the caress like a cat. Her eyes were dark and slumberous. Unbidden, his gaze dropped to her lips, pink and slightly parted. He'd never wanted to kiss anyone more.

"Kiss me," she whispered breathlessly.

Had she said that out loud? Or was it an echo of his own desires?

"I don't think so." He shook his head, as if the potion was clouding his senses too. He was a gentleman. He couldn't take advantage of her in this state. She didn't know what she was saying.

He summoned all his willpower and managed a light teasing voice. "Not until it rains, remember?"

Her perfect lips pouted in comical disappointment, even as she slid one hand around the back of his neck and tried to tug him towards her. Her other hand slid up his chest, and Harry knew she must be able to feel the pounding of his heart through his thin shirt. He told himself to pull away, but he couldn't resist the pleasure-pain of her innocent touch.

He bent and scooped her up in his arms. "Come on, let's get you into bed."

To his surprise, she didn't struggle. He stood, enjoying the feel of her, the heady waft of perfume that teased his nostrils when he moved. He ducked under the tent flap and deposited her gently on her bedroll.

Her arms were still around his neck, their faces so close he could feel the warmth of her breath against his cheek. God, if he turned his head just a fraction of an inch, his lips would be on hers—

Her hand slipped down the front of his chest and stopped abruptly as she encountered a hard, rectangular shape in his chest pocket.

Harry bit back a groan. He'd forgotten that damn thing was in there. He closed his eyes in resignation as she pulled out the silver hip flask he'd carried with him forever.

Her eyes widened at the discovery and her mouth formed a perfect O of surprise. He almost caved in right then and kissed her, just to stop her from drawing a conclusion that would embarrass him.

Damn.

"I gave you this!" she said, a note of wonder in her voice. Her mouth split into a delighted smile. "Years ago. I can't believe you kept it all this time!"

She'd given it to him as a joke one Christmas, filled with his favorite brandy. With her customary dry tone, she'd said it would come in handy to revive all the women who fainted at his feet, or to douse the pistol wounds he'd undoubtedly receive from dueling irate husbands. He'd kept it with him ever since, a reminder of his tart-tongued harridan. It had been all around the peninsula with him, through every battle, every hardship. It was his own personal lucky amulet.

He might not believe in Egyptian curses, like the one associated with that necklace of hers, but he certainly felt safer with the hip flask on his person. He couldn't rationally explain *why*, but he knew he was protected whenever he had it.

He took it from her, unscrewed the top, and took a healthy swig, mainly to buy himself some time. The look on her face—soft shining eyes, hopeful expression—almost slayed him. Surely she'd suspect the depths of his feelings now? His heart pounded madly in his chest at the prospect of exposure.

"Ahh. French brandy. The best," he croaked.

Maybe he should just tell her? Admit that he'd been in love with her for more years than he could count. Admit that he wanted nothing more than to tease her, take her to bed, and let her drive him crazy for the rest of his natural life.

No. God, no. Terrible idea. She was out of her mind on some ridiculous herbal concoction. She wouldn't know what he was saying. She barely knew what *she* was saying. She probably wouldn't even recall this conversation in the morning. Thank the Lord.

She made a grab for the flask, but he fended her off with ease.

"No brandy for you, Lady Morden. You've had quite enough intoxicating liquids for one evening, don't you think?"

She'd managed to wind her arms around his neck again, like an octopus. He gently disentangled himself and stepped back, and she fell back on her bedroll with a little sound of frustration.

"Why don't you just sleep it off, hmm? I'm sure you'll feel much better in the morning."

She frowned at him, her expression crestfallen, and he experienced a gut-punch of regret. She thought he was turning her down because he wasn't attracted to her. Which was ridiculous. But better than the truth.

Knowing Hester, she'd be highly dubious of a profession of love anyway. She'd think he was teasing her, or amusing himself, or only after her money. He didn't know how he'd ever manage to convince her he was serious. *If* he ever decided to tell her, that was.

He opened his mouth to say something to appease her, but she'd already turned onto her side and closed her eyes.

"G'night Tremayne," she murmured. "Go to sleep."

CHAPTER 12

*H*arry covered Hester's sleeping form with a blanket then ducked out of the tent and walked a good distance away. He tilted his head back, lifted his gaze to the stars, and took a deep breath of cold night air.

He was clearly being tested by the gods. Perhaps that damned necklace really *was* cursed. Here he was, being given Herculean tasks, like being made to remain a gentleman when his every thought was decidedly *un*gentlemanly. This, surely, was the finest torture the goddess Serqet—or whatever her name was—could devise. To have the object of his affections so close, so uncharacteristically willing and yet be unable to touch her. It was agony. A plague of epic proportions.

He suddenly wanted nothing more than to stay here in the wilderness. To be lost forever, no maps, just the two of them, and never return to England. To hell with Aunt Agatha, the mummies, and Napoleon. He and Hester could live wild and free, make love under these incredible stars, or snuggle up next to the glowing fire. It got cold at night in the desert. He'd be more than happy to share his warmth.

He expelled a slow stream of air and raked his hand through

his hair. Impossible. And impractical. He liked the creature comforts of modern life. A whole civilized world awaited them back in London.

He glanced back at the tent. Hester had always professed to hate him. Could a mere potion change disgust to love? Surely not. But perhaps it could magnify a desire that was already there. A warm glow of hope kindled in his chest. Maybe it acted like a fan, to turn the flames of a hidden passion into a conflagration. Perhaps she was coming to love him after all.

The fear he'd felt when he realized she'd been stung had been horrific. The wars had taught him the fragility, the miracle of life. He'd lost friends in battle; he could have lost her. Strong men had been felled by a scorpion's sting. In Greek mythology the mighty hunter Orion had been killed by a scorpion, hadn't he? Zeus had placed both the hero and the scorpion among the stars. Harry glanced up again and located the two constellations in the heavens, located on opposite sides of the sky.

Maybe there *was* such a thing as a curse. Hester had almost been bitten by a snake, almost drowned in the oasis, and then she'd endured a scorpion sting. He shook his head, dismissing the fleeting thought. No. It was coincidence; Egypt was a dangerous place, filled with things that could kill you. If it wasn't the heat or drought, it was sandstorms or the inhospitable wildlife. And Hester was a woman who naturally seemed to attract trouble.

Harry couldn't imagine life without her. He needed her to provoke him and challenge him. To entertain him and to improve him. And she needed his protection. He wouldn't dream of curtailing her adventuring—it made her who she was—but he wanted to be by her side, keeping her safe from the Drovettis and scorpions of the world.

The plaintive grumbling of the camel—no, *dromedary*—interrupted his brooding thoughts. Harry gave a deep sigh and headed back to the fire. Tomorrow, if Hester's map was correct, they would catch up with Drovetti. Tonight, he would sleep alone.

CHAPTER 13

*H*ester woke in the morning with a sore ankle and a cloudy head. Her mouth was drier than the desert, and with a groan she sat up and groped around for her water pouch. On the other side of the tent fabric, she could hear Bahaba grumbling and the noise of Harry packing the camp. He was up, then.

Her recollections of the previous night were hazy, to say the least. She remembered being stung by the scorpion, and the pain, and Tremayne giving her the incorrect medicine to drink. She remembered the pain easing and then feeling floaty and flushed.

And desire. Her body had definitely experienced desire. Her friends in the harem had discussed the subject at length, detailing all the physical signs, and Hester had encountered every one of them last night. Her skin had been feverish, her heart had been pounding at Tremayne's nearness. Her stomach had felt all fluttery. Her breasts had ached, as if yearning for his touch. She'd wanted to bury her nose in his neck and inhale the glorious fragrance of him.

Yes, no doubt about it, Uncle Jasper's Blue Nile Lily syrup was an extraordinarily effective aphrodisiac.

A flush of embarrassment warmed her cheeks. Had she made a fool of herself last night? She'd wanted Harry to kiss her, but he'd refused. How mortifying. She'd practically offered herself on a plate. Clearly her desire was not reciprocated. Which meant the only thing to do was to brazen it out, pretend it meant nothing to her.

As always.

With a sigh, she rolled up the map she and Uncle Jasper had painstakingly produced. The Morden family motto, '*Non Perdidi*', stared up at her from the paper, along with her uncle's name. Hester gave a little snort. 'Never lost?' What rubbish. *She* was lost. Not physically, but emotionally. Her heart was lost to Harry Tremayne, and she doubted she'd ever get it back. The only place she wanted to navigate to was into his arms.

Why couldn't she have a map that would direct her to his heart? She knew the answer to that. It was an impossible destination: somewhere as unreachable as the Mountains of the Moon and as inaccessible as the section that said, 'Here be dragons.'

When she'd packed up her meager belongings, she ducked under the tent flap to find Tremayne all ready to go. He helped her dismantle the tent—a simple enough matter of removing the central pole and folding up the striped material into a bundle. They set off.

The first twenty minutes passed in awkward silence.

"Do you know the recipe for that Blue Nile Lily syrup?" he asked abruptly. "Or could you get it from the Bey's doctor, do you think?"

Hester risked a glance over at him to see if he was mocking her. "I could probably get the recipe, yes. Why?"

His lips parted in a delighted smile. "Because it's a foolproof way to make our fortunes." He winked at her. "Well, not for you. You already have a fortune. But for me, certainly. Just think, if it works as well on men as it does women, we'll be richer than Croesus!"

Hester felt an embarrassed flush heat her skin. "Did it have an effect on me?" she said offhandedly. "I don't remember a thing after I was stung by the scorpion. I assumed I'd fainted and you'd put me to bed."

He sent her a sideways glance beneath his lashes that made her heart pound, but refrained from calling her out.

"You've been complaining about me taking mummies back to London," he said. "This is a far more ethical opportunity. I'm certain the fine gents at the Royal College will be fascinated by an effective aphrodisiac."

He gave a chuckle at her horrified expression. "Don't worry, I'll give you and Uncle Jasper full credit. I'll be a silent partner in the enterprise." He waved one hand dramatically across the skyline, as if reading an advertisement on a banner. "I can see it now. Morden's Miracle Medicine. Lady Love Potion. You'll be feted all over town."

"Absolutely not." Hester said stonily. "I'd rather shoot myself."

He took her refusal with a laughing shrug. "Just think about it."

They lapsed into silence again, but as they crested a slight rise, Harry reined in his horse and sent her a look of congratulation. The city of Alexandria spread out below them, circling the port. Hester could make out several large ships moored in the bay. The sluggish green-brown waters of the Nile fed the city, channeled by sluices and dikes that nourished the fertile green fields all around.

Harry pointed. "Look! It's Drovetti."

Sure enough, a group of riders was visible on the road leading toward the town, Drovetti in his hat clearly distinguishable at the front.

"Clever girl! Your map shaved half a day from the journey!" Harry spurred Makeen onward. "Come on. If we follow him we can find out where he's staying. Then we can get back that necklace of ours."

"Of mine," Hester corrected.

Harry just grinned at her.

"Oh, go and take a swim in the Nile," she said crossly.

"Isn't it seething with hippos and man-hungry crocodiles?"

"It is. Take your time."

They trailed Drovetti and his men through the winding streets of Alexandria, taking care to stay out of sight.

"If he's keen to get the necklace back to Bonaparte, he'll head straight to the port and get on a ship to France," Hester said.

Her prediction proved to be correct. They followed the Italian to the waterfront. Drovetti dismissed the men then hailed the captain of one of the ships and, after some hushed conversation, ascended the gangplank and disappeared through a doorway that led off one end of the vessel.

"Now what?" Hester asked.

"We need to get on board that ship." Harry dismounted, and Hester did the same. "Have you any money?"

"Some, but not much."

"We'll have to sell one of our mounts then." Harry glanced from Bahaba to Makeen. "There's no contest. I'm not selling the horse. He's far too beautiful. Your smelly camel will have to go."

"He's a *dromedary*," Hester scowled and patted Bahaba's wooly nose. "Don't listen to him, Bahaba. You're very useful." The ungrateful creature tried to bite her. Hester shrugged. "Oh, all right."

They managed to sell the dromedary to an unsuspecting tradesman in the marketplace, and Harry used part of the proceeds to purchase a pastry pie and some fresh juice from a street vendor. Hester almost groaned at the delicious taste. She hadn't realized how famished she was until she took her first bite.

That done, Tremayne led her into one of the many crowded antiquities shops that clustered the maze of streets. After a fair amount of haggling, he purchased a beautiful, empty wooden sarcophagus.

"What happened to finding your own mummy?" Hester said. "I thought you wanted an authentic body to sell?"

"This is just something showy to get us on board that ship. I can buy mummies for the surgeons later." He pointed to another seemingly intact mummy resting within a decorated case.

"You are *not* taking that back to England to be unwrapped," Hester scolded. "Why on earth do the doctors want to dissect someone who's over two thousand years old? How will that help their knowledge of anatomy? That was someone's grandmother. Have you no respect for the dead?"

He ignored her griping and directed two scruffy-looking youths who were hanging around in the street to pick up the sarcophagus and carry it behind them while he led Makeen back to the docks. Hester trailed behind them, feeling hot and dispirited.

"What are you thinking?" she asked.

He rummaged around in his pockets and withdrew a folded sheet of paper. "I have a letter of introduction from your friend Henry Salt. I'm posing as an unscrupulous antiquities dealer who's transporting mummies back to London on his behalf."

Hester snorted. "That shouldn't be too taxing to believe. You *are* an unscrupulous antiquities dealer."

He ignored her jibe and waved the paper. "This gives me diplomatic privilege to demand passage on any ship in port."

She raised her brows, reluctantly impressed. "Oh."

"Drovetti will probably have gone to find something to eat. I'll distract the captain with my sarcophagus while you go and look for the necklace."

"He won't have left it unattended," Hester said crossly. "He'll keep it on his person."

"That's probably true, but we need to be certain. If it's not there, we'll just wait for him to return and overpower him. I'll hold him down while you search him. But let's make sure it's not in his cabin first, all right?"

Since Hester couldn't think of a better plan, she gave a resigned shrug, but as they reached the docks, they stopped and stared. Drovetti's ship was no longer moored at the water's edge. It was heading toward the horizon.

"Bugger," Harry breathed.

CHAPTER 14

Tremayne squinted toward the disappearing ship. "We'll just have to follow him over to France, then, I suppose."

Hester gasped. "You can't be serious."

"Of course I'm serious. We can't let him get the necklace to Bonaparte. What if there's some truth to that curse? The future of Europe could be at stake." His face creased into a boyish grin of anticipation. "We need to keep Drovetti's vessel in our sights. Come along." He strode off.

"If I didn't know better, Tremayne," Hester scowled, hurrying after him, "I'd think this was some elaborate ruse to get me closer to England so you can claim that five thousand pounds."

He sent her a look over his shoulder. "You wound me. Retrieving that necklace is our patriotic duty."

"You don't think the necklace will grant Napoleon any powers at all. You just love the idea of a treasure hunt!"

He didn't deny it. His eyes sparkled with merriment.

"How long will it take to get to France, anyway?" Hester grumbled. "My clothes are—"

He waved an impatient hand. "Four or five days, I should

imagine, with a good wind. And we haven't got time to get you any more clothes. We have to leave this minute."

Hester sighed. She could hardly refuse to go with him. She didn't want to be stranded alone in Alexandria, penniless, without even Suleiman to protect her. And she wanted to retrieve the necklace as much as he did.

Unlike Harry, she wasn't ready to dismiss the possibly of it having extraordinary properties. She'd felt the strange, heady power of it when she'd put it around her neck, and the thought that she might have been cursed by it, even now, was impossible to forget.

Hadn't disaster followed in its wake as the old man had predicted? She'd been robbed by Drovetti, almost drowned, and then stung by that scorpion. Mere coincidence? Or something more?

If there *was* something more sinister about the necklace, then allowing Napoleon to get his hands on it could indeed have disastrous consequences. The man had already shown himself determined to conquer as much of the world as he could. His hubris and ambition were limitless. With the power of an angry Egyptian goddess behind him, he could well prove unstoppable.

Still, five days of forced proximity on a ship with Harry was enough to make Hester's heart pound. She would just have to do her best to ignore the alarming effect he had on her, that was all.

With Harry's letter of commendation, it didn't take long to find a captain willing to make the crossing to France, and within a surprisingly short time, they had been ushered aboard a tidy brig and shown to separate, adjacent cabins. Not wanting to leave his purchases behind, Harry directed the two boys carrying the sarcophagus up the steep gangplank and onto the deck. Hester watched in amusement as the hapless young men tried to angle it through the hatch that led below. The sarcophagus was over eight feet long and the ladder was both steep and narrow. It took a great deal of gesticulating and remonstrating before the thing was stowed away.

That done, Harry insisted on bringing Makeen, the Arabian, aboard too.

"I'm not leaving such a magnificent creature behind. Just think of the stir he'll make back in England! I can make a fortune putting him out to stud."

Hester rolled her eyes as he persuaded the skittish animal to embark, even as she marveled at the confident way he dealt with the animal.

With the beast finally tethered safely, they set sail. Hester stood at the rail and watched as the haphazard outline of Alexandria's skyline disappeared in a wavering heat haze like a mirage. Would she ever return to Egypt? And what disasters awaited them in France?

Harry stepped up to stand at her shoulder. He leaned easily on the wooden rail and stared out over the water. "No pushing me overboard like you did in Venice," he warned softly.

Hester snorted. "Then don't do anything to annoy me."

She was accustomed to travel by sea. She'd sailed from England with Uncle Jasper. The ship they'd commandeered was a brig, a trading ship with two square-rigged masts. The captain, Jacopo Cavalli, proved to be a portly Italian merchant with a gold tooth and a faintly piratical air. Hester quickly deduced that he was a loveable rogue; he entertained them with tales of his bossy, bustling wife in Livorno and his seven noisy children. He joked that he put to sea to escape their incessant squabbling but then admitted that he missed them as soon as he left port and couldn't wait to return from trading glassware and Egyptian linens for Italian wine and silk.

Signor Cavalli's tales of a loving, boisterous brood made Hester a little envious. She'd always wanted a family of her own. The way the Italian's wrinkled face softened as he recounted some anecdote, the gleam of paternal pride in his eyes as he told of some child's misdemeanor, was evidence of his boundless love.

In an attempt to spend as little time in Harry's company as possible—and thus avoid temptation—Hester made herself busy by putting the finishing touches to her maps of Egypt. Then she re-labeled Uncle Jasper's medicine chest so there would be no repeat of the Blue Nile Lily mishap.

Harry spent lots of time on deck grooming Makeen, scratching the animal's mane, and crooning soft nothings into its flicking ears. Hester refused to feel jealous of a horse. It was only as she lay in her narrow cot at night that she allowed herself to think of Harry in the cabin next to hers, just on the other side of the thin wooden wall. She strained to hear a sound—the creak of the bed or a muffled sigh—but she never heard anything. All noise was drowned out by the rhythmic slap of the waves.

The weather, mercifully, held for the duration of the crossing, and Drovetti's ship remained within sight the entire time. On the morning of the fifth day, Hester let out a little squeal of excitement as the coast of France finally appeared on the horizon.

"Looks like we're going to dock somewhere near Cannes," Harry said, sneaking up behind her so quietly that she almost jumped out of her skin.

She stole a glance at his handsome profile then resolutely turned to study the neat little houses clustering the cliffs around the curved sliver crescent of beach. She'd forgotten just how *green* Europe was. It almost hurt her eyes.

Harry pointed at several large vessels that crowded the bay, and Hester squinted to read the painted nameplates on the side: *Inconstant, Saint Espri't, Étoile.*

"I bet Napoleon sailed from Elba in one of those. And look, there's Drovetti's ship. He can only have a day's lead on us at best."

Hester eyed the townspeople on the bustling wharf in amazement. "Look! They're wearing tricolor cockades on their hats again, just as they did during the Revolution! I wonder if they're newly made or if they just hid them the whole time King Louis was on the throne."

Harry's expression darkened. "I hoped I'd never see such a thing again." He took a deep breath and made an obvious effort to brush off his anger. "Still, it shouldn't be too difficult to follow Napoleon's trail. The locals won't be talking of anything else. Come on, let's get ashore."

In less than an hour they'd unloaded Makeen and their pitifully few belongings. Harry offered Captain Cavalli the painted sarcophagus if he would agree to remain in port for the next few days.

"In case we need to make a speedy escape," he grinned. "Always good to leave options open."

Hester prayed that would not be necessary.

She pretended not to be impressed by Harry's ability to speak French as he conversed easily with the locals, but she'd had no idea he was so proficient at the language. He must have learned it during the war. Her regard for him went up another notch. There was so much more to him than she'd ever suspected. What other hidden talents did he possess?

When she overheard him casually refer to her as 'ma femme,' however, she elbowed him sharply in the ribs. "What did you just call me? Doesn't 'ma femme' mean 'my wife'?"

His smile was thoroughly wicked. "It can mean either 'my wife' or 'my woman'. Which would you prefer? I told them we were on our honeymoon."

His gaze roved her face, settling for a moment on her lips, as if he were considering kissing her to support his fabrication, and Hester's heart gave a thump. His eyed darkened, but she managed to toss her head and break the sudden tension that crackled between them.

"Neither, thank you very much."

He gave her a look that was far too knowing and laughed.

Their efforts to hire a carriage failed. Napoleon had arrived with over six hundred veteran soldiers, many of whom had required mounts, and the locals had gleefully sold even their carriage horses to the 'liberating army.' In the end, Harry was forced to pay an exorbitant sum for a dusty, cantankerous donkey. Despite its comical appearance, however, the animal seemed content to trot along beside the handsome Makeen.

Napoleon, they discovered, had come ashore three days ago and headed northwest, over the Alps towards Grenoble. It was generally assumed that his destination was Paris, where he would wrest back the reins of power from the Bourbon King Louis.

"Look at this." Harry handed her a small printed poster one of the locals had given him. "He's back to calling himself the emperor again."

Hester read the hastily-printed paper, which turned out to be a proclamation from Napoleon himself.

"Soldiers!" she read aloud. "In my exile I heard your voice. I have arrived through all obstacles and all perils. Your general, called to the throne by the choice of the people, is restored to you. Come and join him! Tear down those colors which the nation has proscribed and which, for twenty-five years, served as a rallying signal to all the enemies of France. Mount the cockade tri-color; you bore it in the days of our greatness. I am sprung from the Revolution. I am come to save the people from the slavery into which priests and nobles would plunge them."

She frowned. "Good Heavens!"

"That is a far more polite way of saying it than I would have chosen," Harry said grimly. "But, yes. Let's go."

CHAPTER 15

*T*he next few days were an exhausting blur of hard riding and brief snatches of sleep in tiny roadside inns. The Alpine scenery was stunning, but Hester scarcely had time to admire it, and at every stop Harry's prediction proved true; the only news on anyone's lips was of Napoleon's triumphant return.

They reached Grenoble, only to discover that the city had surrendered without even putting up a fight. The innkeeper reported that Napoleon now had seven thousand troops at his disposal. At every stage his former supporters were coming out of the woodwork and pledging their allegiance.

"Do you think Drovetti's given Bonaparte the necklace?" Hester ventured as they trotted along a rutted, tree-lined track in the direction of Lyons. Every single muscle in her body ached with fatigue, but she refused to complain.

"Probably," Harry said gloomily. "Napoleon certainly seems to be having an extraordinary run of luck." He pressed his booted heels to Makeen's sides and shook his head. "The whole time he was on Elba, he kept promising to stay put, but it was all lies. The man's power-mad."

The possibility that the necklace could be amplifying that desire for power, driving an already-righteous fervor over the edge into a reckless confidence, lay unsaid between them.

"He won't be content to drive King Louis from Paris," Harry continued. "He must conquer. His nature demands it. And the Allied powers will never allow him free rein. We're heading for war, you mark my words." He glanced over at her, and his furious expression softened. "You're exhausted."

He pulled Makeen to a stop, and Hester reined in her donkey.

Harry reached out his arms and indicated his foot in the stirrup. "Come on. Give that poor beast a rest. Makeen's strong enough to carry two for a while, and you look like you're about to fall asleep in the saddle."

Hester was too tired to argue. When she slipped from the donkey's back, her knees nearly buckled, but she managed to tie the animal's reins to Makeen's saddle. Harry hauled her up in front of him and settled her sideways across his lap. Makeen pranced in protest, but Harry controlled him with a squeeze of his thighs, and Hester sighed as she settled against his chest.

She should have felt embarrassed, being held in his arms like this, with her head tucked beneath his chin and her ear pressed to the steady pounding of his heart. But it felt so right, so natural, that she didn't put up a squeak of protest. She simply melted into his body, savoring the spicy scent of him and the hard strength of him beneath her. She closed her eyes with a sigh of contentment. Harry would keep her safe. Harry wouldn't let her fall.

When they arrived at a small hostelry that evening, Harry purloined a newspaper from the taproom and read that the French Marshal Ney, who had promised King Louis that he would convince Napoleon to turn himself in or 'bring the usurper back in an iron cage', had instead turned traitor and returned to Napoleon's side.

Hester couldn't shake the conviction that the evil power of the necklace was coming into effect. The medicine man back at

Kharga had foreseen great destruction, and she had a terrible feeling that things were rushing pell-mell toward some dreadful, bloody outcome.

Luck finally favored them when they rode into the small town of Villefranche. They had finally caught up with Napoleon.

The town was bursting with people who'd come to show their support. According to the local blacksmith, the emperor was staying in one of the larger hotels in town. A great number of wounded officers were being presented to him that afternoon, to receive his thanks and to pledge allegiance to their old commander.

Harry's eyes lit up, and he smiled for the first time in what seemed like days. "That will be the perfect distraction. While Napoleon's busy talking to his soldiers, we'll disguise ourselves as servants, sneak into his rooms, and look for the necklace."

"I doubt it will be that easy. Surely if he has it, after all this time, he won't let it out of his sight."

"It won't hurt to look," Harry countered reasonably.

So an hour later Hester found herself carrying a tray of dirty dishes near the back door of the hotel, dressed as a lowly serving wench. Harry had taken gleeful pleasure in stealing her an outfit from a flapping washing line. She'd been about to lecture him on the ethics of thievery—yet again—when she'd seen him slip a gold coin into the peg bag left hanging there. He was an oddly honest thief.

"Aren't you coming in with me?" she grumbled.

Harry sent her tightly-laced bosom an appreciative leer, and her cheeks heated. She was sure he'd deliberately chosen the most revealing dress he could find, just to make her squirm. Did he like what he saw?

"You make a far more convincing chambermaid than I would," he chuckled, "and I don't want to leave Makeen. Someone might steal him. Besides, one of us needs to keep an eye on Napoleon.

I'll watch him through the front windows and make sure he stays downstairs."

"And what will you do if he looks like he's about to leave?"

"Create a distraction."

Hester lifted an eyebrow. "A distraction."

"I'll pretend to be drunk and start a brawl in the front court-yard. That'll draw everyone's attention."

Hester shook her head.

"I know that's all you think I'm good for," Harry teased. "Don't pay any heed to the fact that I'll be outnumbered ten to one and probably beaten to a pulp. Never mind that some burly French grenadier might snap me like a twig."

"You'll be fine," Hester snorted. "I've never met a man as lucky as you. You always manage to come out of scrapes without so much as a scratch."

He sent her a cocky smile and gave her bottom a playful swat. "Off you go, sweetheart."

Nobody paid Hester any attention as she pushed her way into the kitchens, hiding behind her tray. The entire staff was in a state of mild panic as they scurried to accommodate the demands of their unexpected guest and his huge retinue. Hester exchanged the tray for a pile of clean, folded linens and made her way up the back stairs, looking for any signs that would indicate which room belonged to Napoleon. She passed one set of guards lounging at the foot of the stairs, but they ignored her. Would he have guards standing outside his chamber too? How on earth she supposed to gain access?

She followed a couple of giggling maids along a corridor and stopped with a hushed curse as she caught sight of a huge figure standing guard outside the room at the far end. She turned towards the wall and pretended to be fumbling with a set of keys, then sneaked another glance at the bulky silhouette.

She frowned. It was hard to see against the sunlight, but the man didn't seem to be wearing a uniform, nor carrying a weapon.

He had his arms folded across his chest and he looked . . . oddly familiar. Broad shoulders, baggy pantaloons. Carefully wrapped turban.

Hester turned with a gasp.

"Suleiman!"

CHAPTER 16

*H*er uncle's loyal retainer turned at the sound of her voice.

"Suleiman!" Hester gasped again. "What on earth are *you* doing here?"

A broad smile of welcome spread across the Mameluke's face. "Lady Morden!" he croaked, then cast a brief, fearful glance down the corridor. "Quick! Come!"

Hester rushed forward. Suleiman caught the knob of the door behind him, opened it, and bustled her inside.

As soon as they were alone, he opened his arms wide and pulled her into a crushing bear hug that almost swept her off her feet, then he held her at arm's length and beamed down at her in evident delight. "Praise Allah! Little dove, how is it you are here?"

Hester laughed incredulously. "How are *you* here? I thought you'd been bitten by a snake or fallen into a burial shaft back at Fayium."

Suleiman's black mustache quivered in outrage. "That son of a donkey Drovetti! May eagles peck out his liver. May crocodiles eat his heart! His men attacked me when you climbed into the well. They asked for you, but I say you are up in the hills, making maps. They beat me and bring me to a ship, and we sail here. To France! Drovetti has presented me as a gift to the French emperor."

"That beast! I'm so glad you're all right."

Suleiman's expression darkened. "When I get my hands on him, the snake..."

"Is he still here?" Hester asked urgently. "Drovetti, I mean."

"I have seen him, fawning near Bonaparte, but he keeps far away from me," Suleiman said darkly.

"He's the reason I'm here, too. He stole a necklace I found in the sand near the tombs."

Suleiman's bushy eyebrows rose, and Hester made a waving gesture in the air. "Napoleon is convinced the thing has magical powers."

His expression became intent. "What does this necklace look like?"

"It's rather lovely, actually. A chain with a pendant shaped like a scorpion, set with rubies. I showed it to the healer, and he said it had something to do with an ancient Egyptian goddess named Serqet."

Suleiman's eyes grew wide. "The scorned goddess!" he breathed reverently. "I know of this legend. Madam, he speaks true. It is cursed! Great evil comes to those who possess it. We cannot allow this French dog to have it."

"I quite agree. I was hoping he'd left it in here." Hester cast a quick look around the chamber. "Is this where Napoleon sleeps?"

"It is, but I do not think he would leave something of such value here."

"That's what I told Harry," Hester groused.

"Who is this Harry person?"

"Oh. Ah. Harry Tremayne." She paused, trying to think of an adequate descriptor for the irritating, irresistible brute. "He's an acquaintance from England. A friend of the family. He came out to Fayium to find me."

Suleiman beamed. "I am pleased you have a man to keep you safe. With your esteemed uncle gone, I feared for you, my friend."

Hester laid a hand on his meaty arm. "Thank you."

She crossed to the window and peered out. Judging from the crowds gathered outside, Napoleon was still holding court downstairs. She raked the throng for a handsome black horse and its equally handsome rider but couldn't spy them anywhere. She turned back to Suleiman. "We don't have much time. Can you help us get the necklace back?"

"Of course." Suleiman interlinked his fingers and flexed his arms. His knuckles cracked menacingly. "It will be my pleasure."

"We have a ship waiting at Cannes. We can take you back to Egypt as soon as we retrieve the necklace."

"I do not think Bonaparte is wearing it around his neck, but he is always putting his hand inside the breast of his jacket, as if to check on something. Perhaps he has hidden Serqet's treasure there?"

Hester's heart leapt. "You could be right. We can't get close to him while he is awake, but surely he doesn't sleep with his coat on?"

"The man barely sleeps at all. He stays awake all hours of the night, dictating letters to his poor secretaries." Suleiman indicated a small metal-bound casket on a side table. "He has a box for his hats and another for his pocket watch and other jewels, but I do not think he will store the necklace in there. He will not want anyone to see it. He will keep in his coat. I will try to get it when he bathes tonight."

"Thank you," Hester breathed. "I'll stay close by."

When she slipped back into the darkened stables to find Harry, her heart almost stopped as the tall figure of a uniformed French soldier loomed out of the darkness. She reared back in alarm, her hand on her throat, until she recognized Harry's disarming grin.

"Thought I'd get a better disguise," he whispered. "Vive l'Empereur."

They spent the next few hours waiting for Napoleon to retire. Hester fell asleep against a large pile of hay at the back of the stables and only woke when Harry shook her gently. She blinked sleepily up at him in the half-light. She'd been dreaming of his lips on hers, his fingers stroking her skin. Her body still shimmered with desire.

Harry's face was close to hers. His fingers brushed her cheek, and everything inside her stilled as he leaned closer. His wonderful scent wrapped around her. Still half asleep, she parted her lips in expectation of a kiss, but he merely tugged a wisp of straw from her hair and flicked it aside.

Her spirits plummeted.

"Time to go, sleepy-head," he murmured. His voice was a deep growl that made her whole body vibrate.

Hester rolled away and tidied herself briskly. She *had* to stop imagining things that weren't there.

When she slipped back into the kitchens, she almost tripped over a young lad who was sleeping on the floor in front of the stove for warmth, but he barely roused enough to grumble at her in annoyance. She filled a pewter tankard with hot water; if anyone questioned her, she would say she was delivering a late-night cup of cocoa to a guest.

When she neared Napoleon's chamber, she slowed her steps and was relieved to see Suleiman still standing guard. He beckoned her forward.

"I have not had a chance to search his coat yet, but he sleeps now. I can hear him snoring. I will keep watch while you go inside."

Hester nodded. She held her breath as she slipped inside the chamber and glanced toward the bed for a peek at the man who had brought such strife to Europe.

Napoleon Bonaparte lay huddled in the bed, a rounded lump,

and Hester quelled a wave of disappointment. She'd expected so great a tyrant to be physically larger, but he was a rotund, dumpy little figure. She could just make out his face in the faint moonlight; his skin was pale and his cheeks jowled. He mumbled something, and she ducked down, crawling to the chair where his grey-blue overcoat had been draped across the back.

Her heart thudding in her throat, she slid her hand inside the fabric and felt around for the telltale weight of the scorpion necklace.

There! Her fingers slipped inside a pocket, and she breathed a faint sigh as the necklace slithered into her palm. It glittered in the faint moonbeams that shone through the window when she held it up. She almost placed it around her neck, but then she recalled the uneasy sensation she'd felt last time she'd done that and stuffed it down the front of her bodice instead.

With one last glance at the shrouded figure in the bed, she crawled back towards the door and slipped outside. Whatever Napoleon did now, at least he would not have the power of the necklace behind him.

Suleiman helped her to stand. "You have it?"

"Yes. Let's get out of here."

They reached the stables without mishap and discovered that Harry had saddled not only Makeen but had also managed to find two further mounts from somewhere. Hester decided she didn't want to hear about his methods. She made brief introductions, Suleiman and Harry each gave a brisk nod of acknowledgment, and then they were off through the town.

Hester had no idea what time it was, certainly long after midnight, but the streets were still busy with people staggering out of taverns, brawling, and generally celebrating the emperor's return. A few patriotic songs echoed down the alleyways.

On the outskirts of town, they came across a huge encampment of soldiers, but with Harry's tattered uniform and

Suleiman's menacing demeanor, they managed to pass by unchallenged.

Hester tamped down a wild urge to shout at the top of her lungs as they kicked the horses to a gallop, using the moon to light the way. The necklace was a reassuring weight in her bodice. A great surge of joy filled her, an inexplicable sense that disaster had been averted.

After a few miles they slowed the horses to a walk, and Suleiman drew alongside her. He tilted his chin toward Harry's back.

"I am satisfied with your Harry Tremayne," he said softly.

"The man's a scoundrel," Hester breathed back.

Suleiman chuckled. "Scoundrel he may be, but the man knows good horseflesh when he sees it. And he rides like a Bedouin."

Hester narrowed her eyes at the broad shoulders and slim hips in front of her and tamped down an irrational wave of longing. "Don't tell him that, for goodness sake! He's already insufferably conceited."

Suleiman laughed, and Harry turned in the saddle.

"What are you two whispering about?"

"Just discussing Makeen," Hester said quickly. "Suleiman was admiring him."

"That is indeed a magnificent animal," Suleiman added.

Harry gave the horse's neck a proud pat. "Isn't he, though?"

"I have heard," Suleiman said, "that Arabians are hard to tame. Their nature is wild and unpredictable. They relish their freedom."

Harry sent Hester a slow smile, and for no reason at all, she felt heat rise in her face.

"He is occasionally headstrong, that is true," he said easily, his eyes still on her. "And he sometimes requires a firm hand, but I wouldn't have it any other way. His spirit and stubbornness only add to his allure."

He and Suleiman shared a smile, and Hester frowned. Why

did she have the suspicion they were talking about *her* instead of the horse?

"An animal like that is hard work, certainly, but worth the extra effort," Harry added. "I will be the envy of every man in London."

Suleiman nodded. "It is a precious thing indeed. Take care you do not mistreat it."

Harry's expression sobered. "I would never do that. Such a gift has my undying respect and devotion."

Suleiman regarded him for a long moment and then nodded as if satisfied. "That is good, Englishman."

Hester rolled her eyes at the strange, indecipherable ways of men, and they pressed on towards the coast.

CHAPTER 17

*H*ester had never been so glad to see anything as she was to spy Captain Cavalli's ship still moored at the dockside in Cannes. She, Harry, and Suleiman had barely stopped to eat or sleep for the past two days. They'd slept in barns and in ditches. Meals had consisted of a loaf of bread or hunk of cheese eaten on horseback. The sight of the ship almost brought tears to her eyes. She couldn't wait for a hot cup of tea with milk. And a bath.

Signor Cavalli greeted them like long-lost cousins. Hester staggered up the gangplank and sank wearily onto a barrel on the deck, wanting only to fall into her cabin and sleep for a week.

Suleiman and Harry led the exhausted horses aboard. The ship's crew began to prepare for departure, and someone was sent into the town to round up those who were still ashore.

Hester reached into the pocket of her tattered skirts and withdrew the scorpion necklace. The red gems and reticulated silver glittered malevolently between her fingers. What on earth should they do with it now?

She barely glanced at the figure coming up the gangplank,

assuming it was a returning member of the crew, until she realized the familiar features belonged to Drovetti.

For a stunned moment she could barely think. Had he followed them all the way from Villefranche? How on earth—?

Drovetti gained the top of the gangplank, and his mouth stretched into an ugly smile as he spied the necklace in Hester's lap. He leapt forward and wrenched it from her grasp.

"No!" Hester screamed. "Harry!"

Drovetti turned just as Harry launched himself across the deck and caught the Italian around the waist. They both went crashing to the deck, a tangle of flailing limbs.

Drovetti landed a punch on Harry's ear. With a curse, Harry reared up onto his knees and punched him hard in the face. Hester shrieked, and the Italian howled and fell back onto the boards. Harry straddled his prone form. Drovetti tried to kick his way free, but Harry gave him another quick cuff to the side of the head and reclaimed the necklace with a grunt of satisfaction. It glinted in the sunlight, the scorpion shivering almost as if it were alive.

"Thief!" Drovetti howled. "Give it back! It must go to the emperor!"

Harry stood and stepped back with his prize, his chest heaving with exertion. "Sorry, old man. It belongs to the lady."

Drovetti rose and staggered back a few paces. His nose was bleeding, but a smile stretched his lips as he pointed the muzzle of a small pistol at Harry's chest. He must have had the thing hidden in his boot. Blood dripped off his chin.

"I repeat, Englishman. Give me the necklace."

Harry shook his head. "You don't have the cods to shoot me, Drovetti."

With a sickly smile of malice, Drovetti turned the barrel of the pistol towards Hester. Harry stilled as she sucked in a gasp.

"Now, perhaps, you will do as I say," Drovetti sneered. "The necklace or the lady? Which will it be?"

With a sound of fury, Harry tossed the necklace at Drovetti's feet. It slithered to a stop against the Italian's boot, the red stones shining like the spots of blood which dripped from his nose onto the deck. Drovetti grinned and bent to retrieve his prize, the gun still trained on Hester to ensure Harry made no move to regain it.

And then everything seemed to happen at once.

Suleiman burst out of the cabin behind Drovetti. Hester heard a loud crack and saw a puff of smoke rise from Drovetti's gun. She braced herself for a bullet in the chest, but Harry's muscular body crashed into hers as he shouldered her out of the way. She fell to her hands and knees, and Harry went sprawling onto the boards beside her with a grunt of pain.

Drovetti hurled his spent pistol at Suleiman, but the Mameluke swatted it away as if it were no more than an annoying fly. The Italian made a dive for the necklace and managed to grab it, but with a great roar, Suleiman charged at him. He caught Drovetti's wrist in one of his enormous fists and squeezed mercilessly until Drovetti screamed and dropped the necklace.

Suleiman bent, scooped it up, and flung it over the ship's rail. The silver sparkled as it turned over and over in a wide arc then hit the water with a satisfying splash.

"Nooo!" Drovetti screamed. He shot an enraged glance at Suleiman, leaped onto the ship's rail, and threw himself over the side after the prize.

Hester gazed after him in astonishment. She turned back to Harry to see what he thought of the Italian's foolhardy behavior but her heart caught in her throat as she realized he was still lying flat on his back, clutching his chest and gasping with the effort to draw a breath.

"Harry!" she gasped. "Oh, God. He shot you!"

With frantic hands she shoved his hands aside to see where

the bullet had wounded him. There was a hole in his shirt directly above his heart. Panic seized her.

"No! Harry, don't die! You can't leave me. I need you. I *love* you, damn it!"

She slapped her hand over the wound and pressed down hard to staunch the flow of blood, then frowned. There *was* no flow of blood. It wasn't Harry's chest she could feel beneath his shirt, there was something else there: something hard and rectangular.

Harry jerked and let out an agonized gasp. "Ouch! Bloody hell, that really hurt!"

Hester sat back on her heels, beyond astonished as he sat up with a wince. He reached into his shirt and withdrew a silver metal object. The side of it was crumpled inwards, and the round lead shot from Drovetti's pistol was embedded in the center.

"Your hip flask!"

Hester shook her head, unable to comprehend the lightning shift from Harry being *dead* to Harry sitting hale and hearty right in front of her. "It's supposed to go in your coat pocket," she said stupidly.

Harry sent her one of his heart-melting smiles. "It goes," he said, "next to my heart."

She frowned. Because she'd given it to him? Her heart hammered wildly, but she cautioned herself not to read too much into his words. He was always saying enigmatic things like that.

His mouth curved into that pirate's grin she knew so well. It was the look he always wore when he'd had the last word in an argument or done something that left her speechless.

"I heard what you said." His tone was teasing, his eyes sparkling with mischief. "You *love* me, Hester Morden! No—!" he said when she opened her mouth to argue. "You can't take it back. I heard you, loud and clear. And so did your hairy friend over there." He gestured toward Suleiman, who sent them a jovial wave. "I have a witness."

"But—"

"No buts." His gaze suddenly flicked past her to focus on the sky above. "Well, would you look at that."

Hester turned to see what had captured his attention. An enormous bank of dark, billowing clouds were rolling across the bay with unnatural speed, like a great wave. A rumble of thunder echoed in the distance, and a flash of lightning leapt towards the sea. She blinked in surprise. "How extraordinary."

Suleiman sank to one knee and bent his head. "The goddess!" he whispered. "The sacrifice has been accepted. Her curse is broken."

"Sacrifice? What sacrifice? Where's Drovetti?"

Hester started to rise, but Harry caught her wrist and tugged her back down. She fell across him, her breasts plastered against his chest and her cheeks heated in mortification. She tried to struggle upright but Harry caught the back of her neck and, with a gentle tug, drew her closer.

His gaze captured hers. "I don't give a fig what Drovetti's doing," he said softly. "He can swim all the way to Egypt for all I care."

The look in his eyes—both admiring and hungry at once—made her stomach do a little flip.

Another crash of thunder sounded directly overhead and a fat raindrop landed on the deck next to them, creating a tiny dark stain on the dry boards. Harry raised his brows. His eyes gleamed with humor. A second droplet splashed onto Hester's back, wetting her shirt. And then, as if released from a dam, a deluge of raindrops landed all about them, soaking hair and clothes and skin.

Harry's teeth flashed white as he grinned. His gaze flicked to her mouth and then back up again, and every nerve in Hester's body tingled in sudden anticipation.

"I do believe it's raining, Hester Morden." His breath sluiced over her parted lips. "And *that* means you have to kiss me. A promise is a promise, after all."

"I said I'd kiss you when it rained in the desert," Hester said. She gazed down at him and her throat clogged with sudden emotion. "Oh, Harry, you idiot. You took a bullet meant for me."

His grip tightened on her nape. "Of course I did. I love you. Haven't you realized that by now?"

He didn't wait for an answer. He simply captured her mouth with his.

Hester almost swooned in delight.

His lips molded hers with delicious assurance. His tongue slid along the seam of her mouth, urging her to part her lips, and when she did, he swept inside and took full possession. Sensations swirled through her with the ferocity of a sandstorm. She fisted the material of his shirt and pulled him closer, losing herself in the glory of it.

The taste of him was perfect, wicked and dark, and she wanted to keep on kissing him forever, to play this sensuous game of slide and retreat until neither of them could think.

He groaned into her mouth, a sound of pure animal need, and his fingers threaded through her hair to angle her head to his satisfaction. He kissed her as if he could never get enough of her, as if he'd been thirsting for her taste for an eternity. When he finally pulled away, they were both panting.

"Marry me," he said unsteadily.

Hester shook her head, trying to clear her befuddled thoughts. She released his shirt from her grip and pulled back. "Don't say that. You don't have to offer for me just because we've kissed. I told you that back in England."

He gazed deep into her eyes. "That's not why I'm asking. I *want* to marry you. More than anything in this world. What do you say to one more adventure?"

Hester's heart seemed to expand and glow. "You really mean it?"

He gave a lopsided smile. "God help me, I do. I must be a glutton for punishment."

She couldn't help it; she laughed. He really was a charming rogue. Life with him would never be dull. "We'll drive each other mad."

"I'm sure of it."

"I'll want to strangle you on a daily basis."

"I'll want to kiss you even more often."

"Is that a threat?"

"It's a promise. I'll even kiss you when it's not raining. How's that?"

Hester's smile widened. "In that case, Tremayne, I accept."

Harry gave a whoop of joy and gathered her against his chest. His hug almost crushed her ribs, but she was laughing against his shirt.

When he finally released her, he helped her to her feet, and they both went to join Suleiman at the ship's rail. Hester gasped as she caught sight of Drovetti's lifeless body floating face-down on the swell.

"He drowned?"

Suleiman nodded in disgust. "Crocodiles did not eat his heart." He sounded disappointed. "He went after the necklace even though he couldn't swim. Such is the power of man's greed." He glanced meaningfully up at the sky, which was once again a bright, clear blue, with no hint of the previous storm. "And of the goddess's wrath," he added reverently.

Hester turned to see if the inclement weather had moved inland, but there was not a cloud to be seen. She shook her head, mystified.

Harry was staring out at the murky water, at the spot where the necklace had disappeared. "At least Napoleon won't get his hands on the scorpion. He'd need to dredge the bay to find it now."

A stab of disappointment pierced Hester at the loss of such a beautiful thing, but she shook it off. The necklace could sleep undisturbed at the bottom of the sea. Curse or no curse, she was in no doubt of Harry's love. And that was all she'd ever desired.

Harry glanced over at Suleiman. "Ready to head back to Egypt, my friend?"

Hester elbowed him in the ribs. "You're not planning to buy any mummies to take to England, are you?"

He shook his head. "You made a persuasive argument for not providing the good surgeons of London with—how did you put it? Ah yes,—'somebody's grandmother.' Every time I look at one, I have an image of Aunt Agatha wrapped up in bandages." He gave a theatrical shudder. "No. It won't do. There are better ways to earn a few shillings."

Hester lifted herself on tiptoe and pressed a kiss to his cheek. "Thank you," she whispered.

Harry turned her in his arms and bent to kiss her again, but Suleiman cleared his throat.

"If it pleases you, I have always wanted to visit London. Your uncle spoke of it so often, Lady Morden, that I wish to see it for myself."

"That, Suleiman, is a capital idea," Harry said. "But it's the lady's choice." He glanced down at Hester. "So what's it to be? England or Egypt? I'll marry you wherever you want, you know."

Hester's heart turned over. "London, please. It's time I went home."

Harry flashed a smile at Suleiman. "I can't *wait* to introduce you to Aunt Agatha."

EPILOGUE

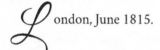 ondon, June 1815.

HARRY TREMAYNE FOLDED down the corner of his newspaper and smiled at his wife as she bustled into the room. He shook his head in silent wonder. *Wife.* He could hardly believe it. He'd finally convinced the irascible, untamable Hester Morden to become Mrs. Hester Tremayne.

He'd barely managed to make it to their wedding without making love to her, but he'd kept a mostly chaste distance during the ten days it had taken to sail from Cannes to London and the three days it had taken to procure a special license from Doctors' Commons.

Aunt Agatha had served as a witness, along with Suleiman, and her smug expression had amused Harry exceedingly. Aunt Agatha seemed to think the wedding was entirely her doing, but Harry had been feeling rather smug himself, as the bridegroom, so he'd said nothing.

The gladness in his heart was echoed by the sound of cheering and celebrating coming from the street outside.

"Have you heard the news?" Hester asked breathlessly. "It's all over town. Napoleon has been defeated! Wellington has gained a famous victory at a place called Waterloo, in Belgium."

Harry put down the *Racing Post*. Makeen had won a hundred guineas on the flat last week at Stamford. He caught Hester by the waist and tugged her down onto his lap. A hectic blush stained her cheeks, but she didn't put up much of a struggle. She wound her arms around his neck and snuggled closer.

"I can't help wondering what would have happened if Bonaparte had still been in possession of the scorpion necklace," she said. "Would it have made a difference, do you think? Would we all be mourning Wellington's defeat and preparing for a French invasion?"

Harry shrugged. "They're saying one of the deciding factors was heavy rain the night before the battle. Napoleon was afraid his artillery would be bogged down by the mud, so he delayed until midday. That gave Blucher's Prussian army time to join up with Wellington's men and carry the day."

"Do you think the curse had anything to do with the sudden rainstorm?"

"Who knows? There are plenty of theories flying around. Someone else said they thought Napoleon relied on an incorrect map, which showed a road where none existed."

Hester raised her brows. "And we all know the importance of accurate maps, do we not?"

"Absolutely," Harry said dutifully.

She put her palm to his cheek. "Do you *really* believe in curses?"

Harry shrugged again. Did he? Perhaps. He definitely believed in miracles. His own particular one was gazing down at him, a wicked expression on her face.

"Come here, wife," he growled. "And kiss me."

She shot a cheeky glance out of the window. "But it's not raining."

"It's bound to be soon. This is England. Think of it as an advance on future precipitation."

She gave a delighted giggle and lowered her head. Harry closed his eyes and savored the exquisite taste of her, the feel of her in his arms. He was home.

After several breathless minutes, she swatted him playfully on the arm. "You're distracting me," she scolded. "I almost forgot. I had a letter from the Royal Society of Physicians."

Harry tried to adopt a surprised, innocent expression and clearly failed, because she narrowed her eyes at him.

"It seems the good doctors are *most* interested to hear about the pain relieving and aphrodisiac properties of a certain Blue Nile Lily syrup I encountered in Egypt. You wouldn't happen to know anything about that, would you, Harry Tremayne?"

A grin split his face. "I know we don't need the money, my love. Not since Aunt Agatha made good with her promise of five thousand pounds to the man who got you back in the country."

She poked him in the chest.

"But you must admit, it would be a shame to deprive the world of something that could be beneficial to thousands. And just think, the surgeons will be so busy researching your love potion, they won't have time to dissect any mummies."

Hester gave a huff, but it lacked heat. She slid off his lap and went to sit at the leather-topped desk in the corner. From the drawer she pulled out a small book, dipped a pen in the inkpot, and began to write.

"What are you doing?"

She lifted her head. "I'm writing a record of our adventures in Egypt."

"Are you going to mention the scorpion necklace?"

"Of course. And the curse, too."

"*Supposed* curse," Harry said.

She chewed the end of her pen thoughtfully. "I know it ended up at the bottom of the sea, but what if it finds its way back into someone's hands someday? A written record of our experience might prove an invaluable resource for future generations."

Harry smiled. "A noble idea. I wouldn't dream of stopping you."

Hester shot him a congratulatory glance. "The perfect response, Tremayne. I believe you might turn out to be quite a good husband after all."

Harry sent her a heated look and enjoyed the pink that tinged her cheeks. "Oh, you know the family motto. *Semper Paratus*. I'm ready for anything you can throw at me, my dear."

THE END.

AFTERWORD

Thank you for reading *The Promise Of A Kiss*. I hope you enjoyed Harry and Hester's adventures as much as I enjoyed writing them!

Please consider leaving a review on any (or all!) of the online retail sites: every review is greatly appreciated!

To see sneak previews of my other books visit my website: www.kcbateman.com. Plus, sign up for my mothly-ish newsletter for regular news, giveaways, and exclusives.

You can also join my Reader Facebook group: Kate's Badasses in Bodices here: https://www.facebook.com/ groups/490385021542157/

Happy Reading!

Love Kate

ABOUT THE AUTHOR

Kate Bateman, (also writing as K. C. Bateman), is the #1 best-selling author of Regency and Renaissance historical romance, including the Secrets & Spies series; *To Steal a Heart*, *A Raven's Heart*, and *A Counterfeit Heart*.

Her Renaissance romp, *The Devil To Pay*, was a 2019 RITA® Finalist. When not writing feisty, intelligent heroines and sexy, snarky heroes, Kate works as a fine art appraiser and on-screen antiques expert for several popular TV shows in the UK.

She currently lives in Illinois with a number-loving husband and three inexhaustible children, and regularly returns to her native England 'for research.'

Made in the USA
Las Vegas, NV
22 October 2023

79491484R10073